BROKEN

by Elizabeth Pulford
Illustrations by Angus Gomes

RP | TEENS
PHILADELPHIA • LONDON

First published in Australia by Walker Books Australia Pty Ltd, 2012

First published in the United States by
Running Press Book Publishers, 2013

Printed in the United States

Books published by Running Press are available at special discounts for
bulk purchases in the United States by corporations, institutions, and other
organizations. For more information, please contact the Special Markets
Department at the Perseus Books Group, 2300 Chestnut Street, Suite 200,
Philadelphia, PA 19103, or call (800) 810-4145, ext. 5000, or e-mail special.
markets@perseusbooks.com.

ISBN 978-0-7624-5004-6
Library of Congress Control Number: 2013938028

E-book ISBN 978-0-7624-5079-4

9 8 7 6 5 4 3 2 1
Digit on the right indicates the number of this printing

Cover design by Robert Williams
The illustrations for this book were created with ink and digital medium.
Typography: Caslon Antique, Futura, and Garamond MT

Published by Running Press Teens
An Imprint of Running Press Book Publishers
A Member of the Perseus Books Group
2300 Chestnut Street
Philadelphia, PA 19103–4371

Visit us on the web!
www.runningpress.com/kids

UNTOLD THANKS GO TO THE FOLLOWING:

*The best little writing group of gals for listening
and offering suggestions: Kath,
Bronwyn, Erin, and Susan
To Katy for reading the first draft
To Sue Whiting—for her ever insightful
and editorial expertise*

THE DAILY TIMES

COURAGEOUS ACTION SAVES THE LIFE OF TODDLER BUT WITH DEVASTATING RESULTS

Jem Wilson, an eighteen-year-old local youth, was killed instantly when his motorcycle slammed into a tree. His sister, fifteen-year-old Zara Wilson, a rear passenger at the time, was taken to the hospital with extensive injuries where she remains in a coma.

According to one eyewitness, the accident occurred when the Triumph swerved to avoid a toddler, who had run out onto the road from between parked cars.

Further eyewitnesses said the child, Marie Suri, would certainly have been killed had it not been for the quick action of Jem Wilson, who is being heralded as a hero by Marie Suri's parents.

Investigations into the fatality on Ross Drive are continuing.

chapter one

My head is full of bubbles. Strange floating words,
bits of conversations, bits of people. Some I know.
Some I don't. Hundreds of colored dots. I can't see
straight. Can't think straight. I seem to be nowhere.
I seem to be everywhere. If only the wretched
thumping in my head would stop.

*"Talk to her. Play music. Read from her favorite book.
Keep everything as normal as possible."*

"You're saying she can hear us?"

*"Unfortunately, that's something I can't answer. But
there is no harm in assuming it's the case."*

"What's going to happen to her?"

"Only time will tell."

A strange light squeezes around the seam of my
head. Squeezes at the constant thump, thump until
it feels like my mind wants to burst.

"Oh my God, Zara."

Mom's voice sounds faraway, almost as if she
hasn't spoken at all, like I've dreamed it, yet I know

I haven't. I reach out to touch her words. They feel damp and sad. Black raindrops hanging on a tree.

I'm fine, Mom. Really.

"It's Dad, Zara. We're right here with you. You're going to be okay. I know it."

"I can't bear it. I can't."

"Yes, you can, love," says Dad. *"We have to for Zara."*

My lovely dad. My sweet mom.

The last drawing I did of them is pinned on my corkboard in my bedroom. Dad is leaning on the open door of our green car and laughing. He is wearing his usual jeans and denim shirt. Beside him, Mom has her arms folded, looking like she is cross. Her black hair is tied back behind her neck, and she is wearing jeans and a yellow shirt.

"Zara," says Dad. *"I'm not sure you can hear me . . ."*

Of course I can hear you. Mom. Dad. Listen. Hello, I yell to them.

". . . I'm going to read to you. Today it's only the headlines in the newspaper. But tomorrow . . ."

He's talking like he hasn't heard me. What's going on?

"It's not fair," says Mom, *her voice full of despair.* *"It's just not fair. That other terrible business and now this with Jem. She doesn't deserve any of it. Neither did Jem."*

Mom's weeping sounds like soft rain on my bedroom window. My mind drifts like it's sleepwalking until there I am. Standing by my window.

I trace my mother's tears with my finger as they run down the glass. Press my burning hot face against the coolness.

From here I can see the path of shells Jem and I made last summer—crunch, crunch—over to the half-built garage. Light steps. Easy steps. I feel myself skipping along.

Then comes another day. The one when Jem got his beloved Triumph.

"Hey! Kiddo," called out my brother. "You want to come for a spin on the bike?"

"You mean it?"

"Why not."

And for a moment our voices are there. As if we had just spoken. As if the words had just fallen from our mouths.

"I know, love. I know. Please don't cry, sweetheart. It breaks my heart."

Dad's voice jolts me, pulls me away from my bedroom window, back to wherever I was before. I don't understand what's going on. I can't think straight with the constant racket in my head. I seem to be shifting in and out of different spaces, different places. Moving between what's in my head and what's not. What's real and what isn't.

"We got through that other business. We'll get through this. Zara is strong . . ."

What's wrong with them? Can't they see I'm all right?

Mom, please don't cry. I wave my arms. See, I'm fine. Truly.

I wait for her to reply. When she doesn't, the noise in my head closes in. It presses against my eyes. Pushes me down into a small space where there's no air to breathe. No space to move. Where it feels like I'm suffocating.

No, I shout. Not there again. Please. Never there.

I smell him. See his eye staring.

I grapple for something to hold on to. Anything to stop me from sliding backward. From sinking into the past.

I won't go there again. I won't.

I try to scrabble back—back to Mom's voice.

But it's too late.

Scars fill the silence and once again I'm a crumpled seven-year-old trying not to cry.

Jem, I yell. Where are you? I need you.

There's no reply.

Just a deep pool of fear tucked inside my head.

Maybe he's snuck out with Alex. No, that's not right. They've broken up.

I try to remember when I last saw my brother. Was it last night? Or was it this morning coming out of the bathroom? But that was yesterday. Not today. Today seems a long time ago now. But how can that be? If it's today, then that's now, isn't it?

I'm getting so muddled.

Then I remember. The last time I saw Jem he was lying stretched out on his bed reading one of his ever so precious Hoodman comics. So maybe he's still at home.

Dad, I ask, where's Jem?

As if I've not spoken, Dad keeps on reading about the survivors of an earthquake in China.

Mom, I shout, where's Jem?

My cry echoes in my ears.

Can no one hear me?

It feels as if I've slipped down between the black and white lines of one of my sketches, that I'm a small insignificant mark on the page. But I am here, aren't I? The hammering in my skull fades. Now there is nothing but a still, moist silence.

Then someone takes my hand. It's Mom. I recognize her gentle long fingers as they curl over my own. How many times has she done that in my life?

At her touch my chest tightens, my heart thuds, and my head begins to hurt really bad. I feel like the past is starting to leak out. But I won't let it. Mom and Dad don't need to know. Not after all these years.

That bit of my life is only for Jem and me.

chapter two

"Is there any change?"

I recognize the voice of Aunt Chloe. Mom's younger sister. With her salon-tinted blond hair, short and sharp. And the family nose. Thin and long like a beak. She's okay in my book.

"Not so far," says Dad.

"She's a fighter."

"That she is."

I can hear them talking. I can feel them around me. Why can't they hear me?

"Have you told her about Jem?"

"What's the point?"

"Surely, she deserves to know."

"No," says Mom. *"Not yet. She needs to get better first."*

"I think it would help to tell her the truth. Say it out loud. On some level she might take it in. You know how close those two were."

We're still close. Jem and me. Aunt Chloe's talking like Jem isn't ever coming back. Of course he is. He's just off somewhere. Temporarily missing. I'll find him. He's most probably stuck in one of his comics.

The strange possibility is there. Then the thought snaps back like a piece of elastic and hits me in the mouth as being totally stupid.

Reading one of his comics, I had meant to say. Not stuck in one, as if caught between the pages.

"Listen, my lovely," says Aunt Chloe, *"once you're up and about, I'm taking you out for the best meal you've ever had. So I don't want any shirking and lying around for too long. This invitation is only being offered for a short time."*

Aunt Chloe's words are blue and watery and sound like upset little waves. I reach out to comfort her. I feel her breath stroke my arm.

Don't worry about Jem, I tell her. I'll find him for you. And before anyone can stop me, I slip away.

A heavy dampness presses against my chest. I need to go back home. That's the best place to find Jem. I walk onto the shell path and my footsteps crunch inside my head. Jem's motorcycle isn't here. I wonder what's happened to it?

We made the shell path together. Jem and me. It was his idea. Shells from the beach, and together we carried them home, the smell of the sea in two old sacks. The day was hot. Sun brilliant, bright. A yellow river streaming down from its parchment of blue.

That day, as I busted the shells with the hammer, I pretended I was hitting that stuck up Chelsea Rawlinson.

"Go for it. Why don't you?" Jem laughed.

Eighteen going on twenty. That's how Jem sees himself. He is smart. But not all the time. He'd been wanting to buy a bike for forever. Cutting grass and hedges and a million other things to get the money.

Not long ago he bought a Triumph. A ratty secondhand one. The muffler shot. Brakes a bit dodgy. He was going to fix it all, no problem, everything that needed doing. I told him he'd be at it months, years even.

A roar rises in my head like Jem revving up the bike. I clamp my hands over my ears.

Make the sound go away. Please. Make it go away. *"Hey! Girl! What's happening?"*

It's Trace. Goddess of the shopping malls. Junkie of flashy jewelry and Gothic eyes. Mistress of extra-short skirts and Facebook. Vampire cell phones and of all things red. My best friend.

"I know, a balloon—it's totally tacky," she says. *"But have you ever been in one of those flower shops? The prices.*

A gold bar would be cheaper."

For Trace to go into a florist there must be something of a crisis.

"Yeah, I know. Normally, I wouldn't be seen dead in one of those places, but, hey, this is different."

I can smell what she's had for lunch. Her usual. A bag of onion chips.

"Anyway, you'll never guess what?"

I wait for her to tell me the latest.

"Only that stupid Ryan's put himself up for the school's pop idol contest."

Having Trace around makes me feel normal.

"Yeah. Thought you'd like that. Ask yourself. What a total dork. Can't even sing. But you know what, me and you should give it a go."

Oh, ha-ha.

"I mean it. We've more chance than that piddling brain Ryan."

A jagged spear of light cuts across my left eye.

"Hey! They said music would be good. So thought you'd like this."

Music from the *Mamma Mia!* movie fills the spaces in my head. Squeezes out some of the dull throbbing.

"You remember us dancing to this? Dressed in those

seventies clothes. Those shoes. Nearly broke our necks."

Trace's voice is over-the-top bright; her words, like fake glass beads, are dropping from her lips and onto the floor.

"You want a sip of juice? Okay. Don't answer," says Trace. *"Just play dumb. See if I care."*

A breeze wrinkles through the room.

It sounds like pages being turned.

I feel myself tumbling over and over, my feet flying in and out of the sky. The blood in my head thudding.

"Jeez, Zara."

Trace's whisper is covered in bruises.

Talk to me, I tell her. Just be yourself.

"Where the shitting hell are you?"

Yeah. That's more like it.

"Give me a sign that you're in there somewhere."

I try to answer, but the hurt sticks pins into my head. Tears pinch the edges of my eyes. My lips are dry. It's like I've been sprinting for days. The inside of my mouth feels like powder, tastes of fine white sand. I'm so thirsty. I'd die for a drink.

"She's going," says a voice.

Something is banging on my chest.

"Stay with us, Zara."

I can't. I've got to go and find Jem.

Jem and me. We've always been good together.

He takes care of me.

The only one who really knows what happened to me when I was seven.

The keeper of my secret.

Now it's my turn to help him.

"Jem," I cry out. "I'm coming."

My steps are light. Easy. Barely making a sound down the long corridor. It's like I'm hardly there at all.

I'm good at running. Always have been. I didn't come first in the hundred meters for nothing this year.

With Trace screaming from the sidelines. "Come on, girl. You show them what you're made of."

Running that race, I was seven years old again, running as fast as I could, running away from *him*.

I waved as I crossed the finish line, arms high in the air.

Then I felt something dripping down my face.

It wasn't raining.

The drips were too warm and salty.

Tears? They weren't mine. They couldn't have been. I'd just won the race.

chapter three

My feet slip and slither in the nothingness. I can't find Jem's bedroom. Around the ring of darkness are small fragments of light. As I near them, I see they are rays of sunlight. I follow one and it's like early morning in our street. Too early for shadows to gather along the cold side of the houses. Too early for any sounds. Too early for the day's weather. Everything is still and quiet, flat like it's been painted, like one of my drawings.

I slip in through Jem's open bedroom window, along with the warm beam of sunlight, and glance around the room. There is no sign of my brother. I was so sure he'd be here. My head throbs just above my right ear.

"Jem," I yell, "where are you?"

I listen for a clue to his whereabouts. But the only sound is that of an angry fly banging against the windowpane. Venting its frustration at being trapped in an unfamiliar world.

I go over to the bed. Pick up Jem's latest comic. He'd been reading it last night. I'm sure about that because I'd leaned over his shoulder and scanned the page with him. Jem had gotten mad, saying he hated when I did that, and told me to go find someone else to annoy.

Staring at the pictures in the comic, I notice something really strange. Last night the window on the second page had been shut. But now the same picture shows the window open. Curtains billowing in a breeze, as if the night has somehow turned into daytime.

I take a closer look.

I see a shadow.

The outline of a boy. Not just any boy. I'd know that cap anywhere. Worn back-to-front with the word *Astro* scrawled across the brim.

It belongs to Jem.

I feel myself rocking back and forth while staring at the cap. How can Jem be inside the comic? I blink and feel something heavy pushing down on me. It's hard to breathe. I sit down on the edge of the bed, the comic clutched in my hand.

What I've seen is impossible. Utterly ridiculous.

I feel a drifting dizziness. My head seems to be splitting open.

The pressure on my chest lifts, my pulse returns.

I flick through the comic's pages, faster and faster. Images fly. Will Jem fall out?

Dumb.

I fling it.

As it hits the wall, I hear the sound of breaking glass.

I go over to where the comic lies, my feet scrunching over small shards of shattered glass. A cold feeling touches the back of my neck.

It can't be.

I pick up the comic. Skim at the page. My skin pricks. I feel sick.

The window at the bottom of the page is shattered.

My hand shakes.

I peer through the fragmented glass and something warm slips through my fingers.

I gaze down.

See drops of red.

I've cut myself.

The blood drips slowly, silently into a hollow well of disbelief.

If Jem is in the comic, says my logical mind, then that's where you'll find him.

But how to get into the comic?

I can't just jump into it. There has to be a way, but how?

Then I laugh out loud. Of course. I can draw myself inside the comic. Isn't that what any artist would do?

I grab my pencil and eraser and begin to sketch the back of myself on the other side of the shattered window. My head with my hair falling over my shoulders. Then my sweatshirt, jeans, and sneakers.

When I've finished, I stuff my pencil and eraser into my pocket and side squint over my shoulder and memorize the inside of Jem's bedroom for when I need to draw it on my return. I see his computer, his untidy desk with stuff strewn on it. A pile of clothes heaped on his chair.

I turn back to the comic. I feel a jolt of electric blue rush through me.

My eyes judder in shock.

My body shakes.

The endless ache in my head eases.

I open my eyes. I'm standing inside the comic, where glass gleams around my feet and, like the shell path, it crackles and crunches underfoot when I move.

Before me stretches a long corridor.

Glistening bright and shining, like the midday sun on the ocean.

chapter four

My whisper crawls out of my throat. Drops from my lips like a thick globule of raspberry juice.

"I'm here." Jem's voice is right behind me.

I swing around.

There is only the corridor. Stretching long like a piece of gum. Anger flares in my chest. "Don't be stupid. Don't play games."

A door bangs close by.

I've got to find that door. If I do, I'll find Jem. I know it.

Blue doors line the corridor on either side. When did they appear? Were they here all the time and I just didn't notice? They must have been.

Which door is Jem behind?

I stand in the glare of the corridor as if drugged. This is crazy—just standing around waiting for an answer.

I came to find Jem and that's what I'm going to do.

I walk up to the nearest door. My footsteps sink into the muggy quiet. Such a strange feeling. The paint on the door looks new. It's not the color of the summer sky. Instead, it's a bright false blue and more hideous than pretty.

I reach for the door handle but there isn't one. What kind of place is this? I stand perplexed. Sweat drips down my back, and my front. It's so hot. I'm so hot. Why don't the doors have handles?

To stop someone getting in.

To stop someone getting out.

Which one is it?

I pull back.

I need a drink. I should have brought my bottle of water with me.

As I stand there uncertain, lost yet not, I feel eyes watching me. I feel their gaze burrowing into my back. It has to be the scorpions. I've seen them in the Hoodman comics. With their long curled tails hiding their secret and dangerous stings. They are the search squad, an army of terror for the evil Morven, Hoodman's biggest enemy. Who kill and collect victims by foul means. Done deliberately to antagonize Hoodman. Lure him into traps.

I PUSH AT A DOOR. IT DOESN'T BUDGE.

My breath comes in spurts. I've got to get out of here. Spots dance before my eyes. It's sweltering. As if someone has turned up the heat. I feel faint. I need to get some air. Need to get out of this airless corridor filled with blue doors and hidden scorpions.

I leave the door and walk.

Now my footsteps sound far away, but I want them back; I want to keep that small sound close. A faint echo crawls through a crack in my head. Like skittering feet.

Stuck in a passageway filled with blue doors, it's like

a long-lost underground tunnel. What's the comic about anyway? Think, Zara. You do know. You've read bits.

Hoodman! The all-powerful good one. The one who saves people from danger. His identity a secret. Not like Superman or Batman. No one knows who he is. Not even his readers.

Hoodman is Jem's favorite comic hero of all time. Ever since he's been little. Not one comic has ever been tossed out. Piles haunt his wardrobe and the tin shed at the back of the yard. He wouldn't even sell any to get the money for his bike.

Hoodman has always had a strange power over him.

"Give it here," he yelled when I snatched the latest comic from his hands the other day. I only did it to tease, to jostle him off his bed, and get him to take me out on the bike. But his face flared with such anger, I dropped it straightaway, stepping back from the fire scorching his eyes.

Jem's never like that.

Right from then, that moment, I knew something weird was going on. Now it makes sense. The answer is simple. He's decided to find out who Hoodman really is. He's given in to his obsession. He's let it overtake him. You can't be that obsessed about something and not have it possess and control you.

"Jem," I cry, "where are you?" My call is sucked up by the creeping quiet. Stolen as it hits the silence.

My forehead wrings with perspiration.

I can't stay here. I'll die. It's just too hot.

"Draw me," said the demanding voice of Trace, not long after she arrived at our school, the memory fluttering like a moth's wings from inside my head. "I hear you're not half bad."

"What?"

"You heard."

Her jaw tilted. White skin, high cheekbones. Narrow, chiseled blue eyes jeweled the Goth pale face and blackness—the heavy, spiky eyelashes and colored-in eyelids. The face that the teachers had given up complaining about.

"Why should I?"

"'Cause I heard you're better than good."

So I sketched her and she liked it.

"Okay, girl. I approve. From now on it's you and me."

Trace has this real crazy way of talking. It makes me laugh. Nobody else has been able to do that. Trace never cares what anyone thinks. And I mean anyone.

The answer comes into my mind easily. To get out of the blazing heat of the corridor, all I have to do is draw a handle on one of the doors.

A round doorknob. Nothing fancy. I pull out my pencil from my pocket and work at it quickly. I need to make it something practical for my needs. There! Done. I grasp the handle. Suck in my breath. Will it work? Carefully, I twist the knob. I hear a soft click. The door opens.

My heart thuds.

I peer into the room. It's empty.

I step inside.

Over to the side there is a window. Air at last. I go over and push it wide open and lean way out. Suck at the freshness. It tastes so good. So cool on my hot face. Droplets from my sweaty face roll down, softly bounce and disappear.

"What have you done?" comes a whisper.

I swing round. There is no one there.

"What have you done? What have you done?"

I crush my hands over my ears. "Nothing. I've done nothing," I yell at the empty space.

"That's what you say, but you know it's not true . . . you know, don't you?" The whisper stings the silence like the deadly hiss of a snake.

I sense something over by the open doorway. I blink hard

and then I see a short man with the thickest head of black hair. It makes him look like a puppet. The sight of him makes me want to laugh. But there's something about him that turns my stomach, so I hold in my laughter.

He steps into the room on spongy soles. He is wearing a white garment, like he's a doctor or something. The door shuts behind him, closing us in together.

"This way," he instructs, his tone soft and persuasive.

Which way? There is no way. Only the door we both came through.

But I'm wrong. The side wall Is a colorless curtain. It only looks like a wall.

PULLED BACK, IT REVEALS A SMALL OFFICE.

PLEASE. SIT.

HE GESTURES WITH ONE OF HIS PUFFY HANDS.

For some unknown reason I do as I'm told. The chair feels totally lush.

"Hey, girl," said Trace, when we were mucking about in LUSH: The Furniture Store Not for the Poor. "Get a load of this. Talk about absolute lush." We made ourselves comfortable in two huge red leather chairs, pretending that we were loaded. We talked in loud voices.

"Are you interested in buying?" said a guy, coming over. His hair like a rooster's plume.

"What! Us?" said Trace. "What do you think?"

"There is a two-week special on that particular suite."

"Really? Have to think about it."

I followed Trace out of the shop laughing. Both of us helpless. My insides falling down with laughter.

Trace always does that to me. You wouldn't know she has a rotten time at home. Not with all the fooling around she does.

chapter five

"I'm here to help you."

Trace and LUSH slide back into the corner from where they escaped. I'm in a comic, in a room I didn't know existed.

"You know where Jem is?" I say, leaning forward a fraction, instinct telling me the man is Morven, even though his chunk of black hair has vanished.

He gazes at me. He reminds me of the big bad wolf in the storybooks Mom used to read. His teeth sharpened to points.

"What color was the door?"

"Blue."

"You're absolutely sure?" His words are slippery and jelly-like.

What's he take me for? "Blue," I say louder this time.

"Good."

What's the color of the door got to do with finding Jem? This person is cracked.

I could rub him out. Just like I do when I get my math wrong. A giggle gurgles at the back of my throat.

"Can you tell me what he looks like?"

I fold my arms. If he doesn't know, I'm not telling him. No way am I going to describe Jem to him. If I do, something bad might happen to my brother. I sit there with clamped lips. The giggle in my throat has long vanished.

"I'm only here to help you."

"I want to find Jem."

"Of course you do."

I knew it. He's not here to help anyone but himself.

Behind me I sense a sinister stirring of the air. A slithering, malignant sound. It has to be Morven's henchman.

I GO TO LEAP UP OUT OF THE SOFT CHAIR. BUT BEFORE I CAN ESCAPE AN ARM CLAMPS AROUND MY MIDDLE.

SQUEEZES UNTIL IT HURTS. I TOSS AND TURN, WRESTLE AND TRY TO PULL AWAY.

It's hopeless. I shout. But I can't hear my words. Where did they go?

"My friend's got a little something for you," chuckles Morven. "Be still. We only want to help you."

"No," I yell. I struggle. Needing to release the steel grip. My head thuds as I thrash from side to side.

Now I'm drifting. I feel the grip on me being released. My head and shoulders slump sideways. I'm falling.

Falling.

It is so peaceful.

Then I hear that hateful scary voice. Morven's. Don't let him take me. Remember something good.

"Rock-a-bye baby on the treetop, when the wind blows the cradle will rock." Mom's soft singing voice cracks. *"How you used to love that nursery rhyme. Do you remember how you wouldn't go to sleep until I had sung it to you at least three times?"*

Where did Mom come from?

"When the bough breaks, the cradle will fall . . ."

I feel her hand on my cheek.

". . . and down will come baby, cradle and all."

Has Morven got Mom under his spell too?

I fumble. Use my right hand to pull out my eraser. My

head is dizzy. If I can get rid of Morven and his henchman, then Mom will be okay.

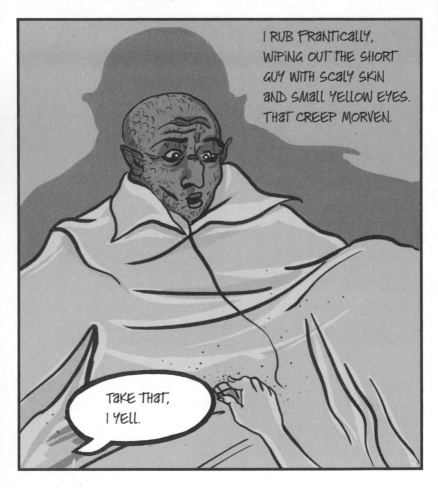

"And this goes for you too. You slime ball." I go to wipe out the henchman, but he's vanished.

"Ha-ha. At least I got Morven."

"There's still no response."

Who said that? I seem to be surrounded by unknown voices.

"Stay with her."

"Rock-a-bye baby on the treetop . . ."

Warm rain falls onto my face. Or is it Mom crying? Don't cry, Mom.

"Don't ever tell me what I can or can't do. You hear me," I yell to the erased Morven, as I get out of the stinking office with sides that squeeze until I can't breathe, until I can't talk.

Once I'm back in the corridor, I laugh. Morven and his scorpion crew think they're so smart. If they were, I wouldn't have been able to wipe Morven out with my eraser the way I just did.

I start to walk. My legs shiver. They want to sink down.

I spot a figure in the distance. I squint. It looks like Jem.

"Jem," I yell. Not caring who hears me. Not caring about anything now. I'm so close to him. It's only a matter of time. I need to hurry, catch him up before he vanishes again.

I run. Down the everlasting corridor, my arms outstretched, as if trying to grasp the silent, shadowy figure.

Then he vanishes. Just like that. He's there one second and gone the next.

I blink and blink. It was Jem; I know it was.

Now there is nothing. Only the return of the dreadful dull thrumming in my head. I want to bang it out. Put my head on the ground and bang and bang.

My legs have stopped moving. I let myself slide down the wall to the ground, closing my eyes against the ever-seeping sludge of tiredness. If only I could sleep. Then the noise in my head would go away. And the blue doors.

chapter six

"Hey, girl. You going to lie there forever with me talking to myself?"

Doesn't Trace know how exhausted I am? Why doesn't she just leave me alone?

"Remember that time we skipped school? Man, did we nearly wet our pants."

Do I remember? How could I forget? Me and Trace off to the beach for the day to meet two guys. We'd never done that before—not turned up for school. I'd had boyfriends though. But not then. Not that day. Thanks to Chelsea Rawlinson.

"And, hey, with you trying to walk in heels on the sand. Jeez, girl, you looked totally grim. But what a laugh, eh? Me wearing those shorts, tighter than a bee's bum."

The sea smelled strong after the night's storm. Seaweed lay strewn everywhere. The two guys were older than us. It was Trace that arranged the whole thing. Hooked up with them online. It was a first for me. I did it because I wanted to get back at Paul.

Though when my online guy wanted more than a bit of kissing, his hands rough all over me, that's when I took off. Tried to run in those stupid heels.

"Dumb when you think about it," says Trace, "but bits of it were fun, you gotta admit."

Yeah.

But not the despair from Mom over what I did. Nor Dad. Despair and stupidity over what I was turning into.

Jem just laughed and said it would teach me a lesson and that there were plenty of other ways to get guys. And didn't I know that Trace played me? Then he went back to reading his comic.

I loved him for that. For not yelling at me. Not saying it was because of what happened to me when I was little.

Like all the others did and still do.

So, yeah, bits of that afternoon on the beach were fun.

chapter seven

A prod. Right where my arm hurts. I move. Roll
over, curl back into the sleep ball.

Another prod. This time it is firmer.

Please go away and leave me alone.

Then I remember. Jem. I'm meant to be finding
him. Not lying in some corridor feeling totally
wiped out.

"Hi, Zara."

I'm wide-awake at the whisper in my ear.

It's Paul. My heart jumps. You've come. I'm so
glad. I thought you hated me after what I did to
you. To us.

A hand brushes my own.

Then I know it's not Paul.

Tears well; the same ones that have nowhere
to go.

"It's Brian. Brian Hamlock."

I picture Brian, a year ahead of me, who I know
has a bit of a thing for me. Tall with spots on his

face and long, thin hair. A gawky guy with big feet, who always manages to look untidy. But after the first time he played the piano at assembly I stopped thinking he was a total twit, because he was totally brilliant.

"I'm really sorry about what happened," he says.

In my mind I see him hunched over the piano. Beethoven spilling from his long fingers, spiraling up and through the strands of his thin hair, soaring up to the rafters of the school hall.

The tune changes. It goes sad. Brian has gone. Now someone else is bent over a piano. It's Mom. She used to play years ago. Now she hardly ever does. She wanted me to learn and I tried, but I just couldn't. It wasn't me. Art's my thing.

"Your mom said that music would be good. I don't know what you like, but this is one of my favorites. It's Mozart. His Piano Concerto no. 21 in C Major."

I have never really listened to classical music before, except on the odd occasion when it was forced on us at school. I always thought it was dumb, boring, but now, its hypnotic power is haunting a part of me that has been hidden for a long time. The notes dropping into that summer afternoon when I went missing.

A swishing sound fills the corridor. A warm barrel of wind gusts through the passageway. I'm tipping, rolling, head over heels.

"Hold on," a voice tells me.

To what? There's nothing here.

TUMBLING. DUST AND DIRT FLY INTO MY FACE, MY MOUTH.

It tastes and smells of ink. Or gasoline. I'm carried along like an insect in a storm. Then it all stills.

I LAND WITH A CRASH AGAINST THE WALL.

My body slams against the stones. A pale light beams into my eyes. A warm, sickly heat covers me. I feel so rotten. Now I'm shivering. Shaking with cold. I try to wrap my arms around myself but the right one isn't there.

"My arm," I scream. "Where is it? What have you done with it? It's mine. Give it back."

"Her right arm took the full force."

"Will she be able to use it again?"

It sounds like Mom.

"In time."

"Did you hear that, Zara? You'll still be able to draw."

I've been drawing already. So what's Mom going on about?

I stare up at the rounded ceiling of the tunnel.

She must be teasing.

I shook my head as Trace teased a bunch of guys while wiggling past them. Deliberate-like. And like wolves, the guys showed their sharp teeth of prey and licked their drooling lips.

"One day you're going to get it," I said.

"Bring it on," was her response. Her heavy black lips snapping at the air.

Trace told me that her dad tried to punch her

once. He didn't get far. She kneed him in the right place. He's left her alone since then, she said.

chapter eight

Before, the walls of the comic were smooth and white, now they are gray and full of gristle. My arm is pinned down by something heavy. I can't seem to move it. I need to get out of this passageway. I need to find Jem so we can both go home. I twist my head. Behind me it's dark, black, and heavy.

Then I know what's just happened. Someone's turned the page of the comic. That's why I went flying. I'm caught on the page beneath the one with the smashed window. The page where I drew myself into the comic. It seems so long ago now. I feel like a squashed fly between the two pages. The same as all the flies I squished and put in Gran's underwear drawer in payment for all the "don'ts."

I spit. It's black gunk.

"Here," says the same voice that told me to hang on.

I see an outstretched hand. I take it. Feel myself being gently pulled, feel my stuck arm released. I'm lifted away from the stone wall. My hands are covered in scratches. Deep gouges. Blood drips.

"You've got to trust me," he says.

Just as Paul trusted me.

THE STRANGER PULLS ME UP. I LOOK CAREFULLY AND FOR THE FIRST TIME I SEE HIM.

There's something familiar about him. What is it? Where does he fit into the comic? He's wearing an odd outfit. As if it's been painted onto him, like streaks of feathers. Colors from the underbelly of autumn, the darkening sky in a thunderstorm, veins of silver. I could have sketched him. Did I? No. If I had, when did I do it? Besides, I only have a pencil. No colors. He simply appeared.

I remember all my drawings, paintings, and sketches. They are part of me. They come out on their own. A side of me that remains secret until I sketch. It's not like I have to think about what to draw. Last year my teacher told me I'd make a good writer. And one day I might try it. Even write down what happened to me when I was seven. Exactly how it was. But for now, I really don't care about reading or sticking words down on paper. Too boring. I like pictures. Once I start on a drawing it's like I can't stop. I'm pulled into it and can't get out until it's finished. It's weird, but true.

The stranger's face in the comic is kind looking. He has brown eyes, dreamy. Very like Paul's. Trust me to muck up things with him. One of the best things in my life, and the best-looking guy at school. But it seems like I'm always doing it. Sabotaging my own life one way or another.

At first Trace was jealous of Paul. She didn't need to tell me. Nobody did. I just knew. But she didn't make me go off with Jack to the park. That was me being totally dumb. It was really nothing, the thing with Jack, but I made it into something. Secretly, it was a test to see how much Paul really cared. That was how it started. Then it was too late.

It gave Chelsea her chance to simper up to Paul and tell him all sorts of things, especially what I had been up to. Of course he believed her. Why wouldn't he? When it was the truth. So Chelsea got Paul while I got Trace back full-time.

Smashing shells that day with Jem while making our path helped deaden the pain of my stupidity.

"What do they call you?"

"Dark Eagle."

Hoodman's greatest friend. His savior. He's never really seen. Always only the outline of large wings. Powerful yet mysterious. Dark Eagle is the one who saves Hoodman when he's in trouble. That's why to me he's the real hero of the comic.

Strange though that he's here in color. In all the Hoodman comics I've read, Dark Eagle's always been my favorite character.

"You want to find Jem?" says Dark Eagle.

"Where is he?"

"He's with Morven."

"He can't be. I got rid of Morven."

We're moving now, along the corridor. It's like my feet are motionless, but at the same time I'm sliding along effortlessly. Dark Eagle is nothing more than a shadow.

Soundless, slipping in and out of his colors. Weird.
Hypnotic.

"Morven's got more than one way. These being known
only to himself." He pulls me to a halt. His touch is light. His
voice hardly there at all. A stealthy whisper slipping through a
crack in a door, a crack in my head.

Before me lies the long white corridor and the blue doors.
Hundreds and thousands of blue doors. What's behind them
all? More Morvens?

Even though the page has turned, it feels as if it hasn't—
like nothing's changed at all.

Where's Hoodman? Why isn't he helping to find Jem?

Because he wants Jem for himself, answers my mind.

The questions and answers roaming in my head sound like
someone typing on a keyboard.

I STRAIN TO FOLLOW HIS GAZE. AS I DO, I SEE A SHIMMERING IN THE DISTANCE. IT LOOKS LIKE DAYLIGHT.

It has to be. My mind weeps at the thought. I hate the blue doors. I want to break them down.

Why don't I draw myself outside?

"You can't," comes the answer.

How did Dark Eagle know what I was thinking?

"You'll never find Jem if you do."

"Where is he? Show me."

"Look to the third door."

I turn.

Warmth stirs beside me. Dark Eagle's gone. Vanished as if he was never here.

I'm alone again.

The third door starts from where? Here? Opposite? Behind? Farther down?

I take my chance. Try the third door on the right. My fingers stretch out to push.

"What do you reckon?" yelled Jem.

His leather jacket felt safe. Smelled safe. My arms clung to his middle. Shadows flew through us. Bits of branches sliced through the sunlight.

"Great." My reply lost against the growl of the bike.

My body was humming. The sound of the engine made music in my mind. Now we were sailing across the sand. Skimming as light as a newborn wave onto the beach. Crushing shells. Spinning up the beach. Scattering seagulls. The roar of the bike and the howl of the waves blew through my ears, my hair, and my laughter.

"Watch out for the seaweed." My words are torn from my mouth and tossed into the air.

The bike leaned, swerved.

Sand flew up, spat out our side like a rip.

I laughed out loud.

It was totally the best feeling.

chapter nine

"*Why didn't you tell me? Did you think I wouldn't ever find out? Did you think I'd laugh or something? Did you think it didn't matter? Do you think I don't matter that much?*"

I know what's coming. I close myself off against the truth.

"*Shit, girl. Getting kidnapped is no joke.*"

How did you find out?

"*And if you're wondering how I found out, your mom told me. She was crying and it just came out about how you'd gone missing when you were seven. For six weeks. Six weeks and they hadn't a clue where you were. Jeez, even my stupid family couldn't handle that. What a messed up thing to happen. I'd have scratched his eyes out. Yanked his bits . . .*"

So now Trace knows.

"*. . . you poor, poor kid. Hell. What you must have gone through. Talk about crap happening. You should have told me. Wish you'd told me.*"

Don't go on about it. Don't feel sad for me. Just don't. Okay? I don't want to talk about it. Ever. You hear me? Not ever. Ever. Ever.

"Criminals like that should be locked up and the key thrown away."

I close my ears. Don't listen. Now Trace will feel sorry for me. All the time underneath everything, every time we meet, every time we're together, it'll be there. That sadness. I don't want it.

That's why I didn't tell you, I yell at her. That's why. So leave it. Just leave it where it was. Pretend you still don't know. Okay?

"Those kind of folk should be all put together on an island so they can get on with it."

Silence settles between us. It is filled with sickly yellow smells like the stinky daisy bush by the front gate. And the cheese that Mom bought once to try out. What a stench. The only place it ended up was the trash.

"You want some of this grape juice? Nah, didn't think so. You don't mind if I do?"

I want to laugh and cry all at the same time. Trace is back to herself.

Doors.

Doors to heaven.

Doors to hell.

Doors to houses.

Doors to cupboards.

Doors to darkness.

My fingers burn when I touch the door. I snatch them away before they fry. Again there's no handle. It seems Morven and his crew have got wise to my last trick of drawing in the doorknob. They have poured on heat to make it impossible. I kick the door with my foot. It flies open and then swings shut again.

To get inside the room I need to be cunning. Sneak through without the door touching me. That way I won't get burned.

I take a deep breath and suck myself way in.

Now I am a skinny shadow.

I am flat like one of my drawings lying in my sketchpad.

My foot hits the door.

WHAM.

It swings open. Wide. Wide. Yawns all the way.

Now!

I dive through the opening.

The door comes at me. I move sideways but I'm too late. It grazes my shoulder. An acid stink fills my nose. It makes me cough; I clutch at my throat.

The door slams behind me.

It sounds different. More solid. I'm locked in.

I know it without checking.

Like I knew how many nights Mom came into my bedroom to check on me when I was back home after I went missing. How she just sat there.

And how her tears kept falling onto my duvet cover. Falling like they were never going to stop.

That's what the person who took me did to her.

I'm in the room. On the tables are trays filled with gear. Needles, syringes, bottles of pale liquid. Instruments of all descriptions. A rank smell rises from them. A kind of sterilized smell. It turns my stomach. Seeps up my nose and I can't get rid of it.

I move away from the table.

Jem's not here. There's no sign he's ever been here. No sign that anyone's been here for ages. It's as still as the middle of the night. Dark Eagle was wrong.

It's hopeless.

"Jem, where are you?" I sink to the floor. It's all too hard. My head hurts. Why doesn't the thudding stop? Make it stop. Someone. Please. I clutch the ache and rock back and forth.

"Here, sweetie, let me help you."

Aunt Chloe picked up the skateboard. It was a present for my eighth birthday.

"I hate it," I told her. "Take it away."

"Sure." She walked over to the half-finished garage. Dumped it under a tarpaulin then came back to me. "There. All gone."

But it wasn't.

And it still isn't.

Not that horrible way-down feeling in my stomach. Not the shivers. Not that scared feeling hiding inside me. Not the feeling that I'm not really here. Not anywhere. That seems to stay no matter what anyone does for me. No matter what anyone says to comfort me. It stays all the time. It's with me when I go to school, and when I come home. It's there when I'm sitting at the table with Jem, Dad, and Mom talking. It's there through the night. It hangs around my bedroom and the things which I used to love.

I don't cry though. I'm good at not crying. Instead, I bite my tongue. I learned it's better than crying. My tongue is sore a lot of the time. But no one sees that. No one looks inside my mouth at where I keep my pain.

A small draft creeps around my ankles. I shrink against
the wall.

The door's opening.

Please let it be Dark Eagle.

"There. There."

I want to vomit.

It's Morven. But it can't be. I got rid of him. Rubbed
him out. But what did Dark Eagle say? That there was more
than one? Or that Morven had more than one way? I just
can't remember.

That's okay. I'll get away from him. I did it before. I can do it again.

He walks toward me. His horrible yellow eyes staring at me, trying to suck me in. I blink several times. He will not hypnotize me. He will not. I feel myself swaying with tiredness. I want to lie down. Leave all this behind. Find Jem so the two of us can go back home.

"You don't scare me," I say, sticking out my chin.

"I'm not here to scare you. I'm here to help you."

Yeah. Yeah. You and all the others. I don't need any help. You got it? I'm fine. How many times do I have to tell you? You hear me.

I'm screaming, but there's no sound.

"Tell me what you did, what happened; it will help you to find Jem."

Ha! I'm not fooled. That old trick. Stick it. You're after Jem as well. You think he'll tell you what you want to know, but he won't. And you're not getting anything from me. You think I'm dumb. I know what happens if I talk to you or anyone else. The woman who took me told me. Her, with the fat lips and eyes of water, like she was always crying about something. That's why you're not ever going to get anything from me. I learned not to talk when I was little. It's easy when you know how. So you can try to persuade me all you like. I'm not telling you anything.

"I want Jem," I say.

"Later."

"Now." I stare coldly at him. Glare at him with intense dislike.

"Wait here."

Of course I'll wait here. There's no escape. There's no window in this room.

The door slams shut. I know where he's gone. He hasn't gone to get Jem. He's not stupid. Neither am I. Morven is evil.

I go over to the wall, the one farthest from the tables. I need a way out.

THEN WITH a GRIN, I QUICKLY SKETCH a WINDOW.

I haven't much time. Now to draw something on the other side of the glass. But what? A garden. Too complicated. Somewhere soft to land when I make my getaway.

I sketch in tufts of grass.

That'll do.

I push open the window and scramble through. I land in a heap on my scribbled grass. As I jump up, I hear Morven's voice. Without hesitation I rub out the window.

"She's gone." Morven's anger stings the air.

Ha-ha. I laugh. Fooled you again.

Jem always says I'm smart. Not smarter than him. But pretty clued-in.

The grass is coal colored, not green like normal. Everything is black. It's only that way because it's in pencil.

But it doesn't matter. Color's not important here. At least I've escaped the blue doors.

My throat is dry and I need a drink. But where . . . ?

Silly me. I keep forgetting.

I draw a fountain a little way off. Have water tumbling, spilling out and over the top of a fluted spout. It is murky charcoal. Still it's something to drink. I take a handful and gulp it down. It tastes good. Even though I drew the fountain in a hurry, it's not half bad. Quite pretty in fact. I trail my hand through the cool liquid. A sticky substance stains the water.

Blood swims like a thin snake from my wrist.

Trace is always in trouble at school. They have kind of given up on her. They've stopped fighting her Goth look. The powers that be have decided it's better she's at school looking like a ghost, than not there at all. But it's not fair. If someone would give her a chance, treat her like something other than a disturbance, she'd be great. But she doesn't care what they think of her at school or anywhere else for that matter. She puts herself right in it with the teachers every time. Especially, Fran Winter the math teacher. Fran is young and full of herself. Most of the kids don't like her. Rumor has it that she's just filling in time until some film studio spots her, which is hardly likely to happen at Riverstone High. Trace is brilliant at math, but she won't let anyone know. Ms. Winter and Trace have been at one another's throats ever since Trace started at the school eighteen months ago. It's like Trace wants to be expelled. And no guesses who does my math, giving me top grades. Yeah. Trace. And yeah I know. What's going to happen when the exams roll around? Hopefully, I'll scrape through.

But it's no wonder Trace's got a disruptive attitude. You would too if you had to live the way she does. With a layabout father, a real tart of a sister, and sad person for a mother.

Trace is an accident. "A bloody accident." That's what she told me. Said she's heard it enough times. Said she doesn't care. Why should she? That's why I like her. The two of us have stuff in common.

Morven and his scorpions are on the losing side. He can keep at me all he likes. He's going to get zilch.

I know when it's good to keep my mouth shut.

And that's always.

Because the man told me what would happen if I didn't.

chapter ten

"Hello, Alex. How nice of you to come."

Why is she here? She and Jem broke up ages ago.
She dumped him. It wasn't Jem. He's still really into
her. Alex with her short, black hair fanned over
her skull like a cap. Tall, gracious, seventeen, and
heading to be a lawyer.

Because of that, the lawyer bit, she doesn't want
to get tied down. She wants to experience different
relationships, not just one. Stupid cow. She needs
to see what she did to Jem. Sitting in his bedroom
for days on end, staring at nothing or reading his
comics. Mom and Dad held hushed meetings using
words like "counselor" and the "s" word.

I know Jem better than they do. Know he
wouldn't go and kill himself. Not after buying his
bike. But Mom and Dad set up watch. It was so
obvious. Using all sorts of excuses to hover near his
room, check in with Jem every now and then.

Not that you could blame them.

So, Alex, you really need to know what you did. Not only to Jem but also our parents. How you dealt out a hand of fear for them. A deck of cards: life, life, death, death. Which one? All for your freedom.

I know it was your choice. But you hurt Jem really, really bad. Not that he's shown it to anyone. But he couldn't hide it from me.

"I came as soon as I heard," says Alex. "I am so sorry. Really I am. About everything."

"It's okay," says Dad. "It's nice of you to come. How are things with you?"

"Fine, thanks." Alex's voice is breathless, as if she can't find it, as if it's slipped down the side of her mouth and lodged itself there.

"I didn't know if she would need . . . what she would need . . . so I brought some orange juice."

Alex smells like the garden after summer rain. Fresh and clean. A lily-of-the-valley kind of smell. I recognize the perfume from those flowers. Mom hates them. There's a patch round the front that keep on multiplying. No matter how many she pulls, digs out, underground the roots keep on traveling. It makes Mom furious and she threatens to poison the whole lot, except she's got some peonies nearby and she doesn't want to risk killing those as well.

My wrist has stopped bleeding. The cold water has done the trick.

I get up from the fountain.

I'm in a place of my own making. I've sketched myself into the white edge of the page. I need to get back into the actual comic. Back through the window I drew, then rubbed out.

In the blackened grass I see imprints of where I landed.

I sketch a window.

Stand on my tiptoes. Peer inside the glass.

Whatever was in the room has gone.

So I'll make it as it was. I put in as much as I remember about the room. Tables, chairs, instruments.

I add the door last. I remember that okay. Now I need to get in and out of the room before someone finds me.

The window is stuck fast. Tight against the invisible wall.

Dumb me. I should have drawn it open, the way it was when I leaped out.

I rub out the frame of the window.

Feel the time ticking away.

I have to hurry.

Otherwise it's going to be too late.

I'm not sure why it's going to be too late; I just feel it.

I scribble away. Now the window is open.

I clamber back inside.

After landing with a thump onto the floor, I pick myself up and dash over to the door.

I BASH IT OPEN WITH MY FOOT, REMEMBERING ABOUT THE HEAT, AND SLIP THROUGH BEFORE IT CLOSES ON ME.

I'M BACK IN THE PASSAGEWAY WHERE THE DULL HEAT CRAWLS BACK INTO MY HEAD.

I begin to walk. The passageway can't last forever. Nothing lasts forever. At least that's what Mom tells me when I'm having a hard time.

chapter eleven

"Hey, girl. How's it going? Yeah. Thought so. Still lying around taking it easy. Anyway," Trace says, lowering her voice, *"I'm going to tell you something. It's a bit shitty, but I reckon you of all people should know."*

I can't imagine what Trace is going to say.

"Seems like that weird guy who lives a couple of blocks from you was pulled up for trying to make off with a kid in the park yesterday."

I don't want to know. I'm not listening.

"Apparently, the kid's dad spotted what was happening just in time. The guy denied everything of course. Said he was just helping the little girl find her ball. Yeah, right!" Trace splutters. *"Suppose you're wondering how I know all this? Family connections, you might say. Dad's got a nose for sniffing out this stuff."*

My head feels as if it's shaking from side to side.

"I'm telling you this because I reckon he had something to do with you when you went missing . . . people like that never change." Trace is silent for a few seconds and then

starts up again. *"He looks all respectable by working in an office in the city somewhere, but I heard he's into cross-dressing big-time and that he's a real mama's boy."* Trace makes a gagging sound. *"Dunno who told me all that, but I believe it. He's one totally strange dude."*

Inside, I'm heaving as if I'm about to throw up.

"Someone like him needs to be locked up."

My stomach quiets as my mind shifts. It floats over what Trace has said. I am examining her words, picking them up, studying them in a cold-hearted kind of way to see if they belong to me. They don't, so I leave them in a pile and return to myself.

"Even my dumb family doesn't do stuff like that."

By that Trace means her dad was more into the occasional robbery. While her sister did a bit of hustling on a street corner on a Friday night to get some quick cash.

First time Trace told me all this, I didn't believe her. I nearly walked away from her so she couldn't mess with me. Trace didn't get mad. She laughed and took me to the rough side of town and there was Selma, just like she said. Dressed in a bit of a skirt with boots climbing up to her thighs, strutting up and down. When she saw Trace mimicking her, she shouted, "Piss off."

"My charming family."

"You wouldn't ever, would you?"

"Give us a break. Dad gets me everything I want."

I had wondered how she always had the latest cell. Along with all the other electronic gear.

At last I can see the corridor coming to an end. In the distance it's branching off in two different directions. Both splits in the passageway appear the same. I pause and try to decide which way to take.

The air is stifling. It presses against the back of my eyes. My feet ache and so do my legs. Mostly my right leg. I glance down. The lower part of my jeans is soaked. I touch it. It feels wet and looks like black ink. I know it can't be ink so it must be blood. I haul up the material. There's a long gash. When did that happen? It must have been when I was getting back into the room through the window. Funny that I didn't feel it before. I need to stop the bleeding. I need a cloth of some kind.

If I go back to the room from where I escaped, there might be a rag or something I could use. But which door was that particular room behind? No—I'm not going to go backward, it's better to keep moving forward.

With no other option, I sink my teeth into the lower edge of my T-shirt. The material is tough but not impossible. A section tears off. Mom is so not going to love me for doing this. But it's better than bleeding to death. I wrap the fabric around my calf, pull it tight. It feels as if I'm squeezing my leg to death. But I don't stop. Tighter. Tighter. Just as we were taught at school. The first-aid class where Trace and I acted like fools. Bandaging ourselves to look like Egyptian mummies, up until we were sent out of the class.

My head swims. The heat so unbearable, I feel faint. I'm blacking out, and there's a scream caught at the back of my throat that won't move. It's full of reds and browns and yucky yellow bits. All stuck there. My breath comes in spurts. I try to suck in more air but it can't seem to get past the locked-in scream.

"What's happening?" whispers Mom.

Air fills my lungs. I breathe again.

"Good," says the soothing voice. "She's stabilizing."

I feel my hand being rubbed.

"Please, Zara. You can't leave us. I need you." Mom's voice sounds so distraught that I almost decide to give up searching for Jem and stay, but in the end I know it's important to find him.

"She's okay now."

Mom strokes my head, the strands of my hair falling through her fingers like a warm breeze.

I'm sorry, Mom, but I really need to go and find Jem. I won't be long, I promise.

Now which is the best way to go?

Left or right?

Both look the same.

In the end I choose the direction leading to the right.

chapter twelve

I feel moisture. As if someone is pressing a cool cloth to my forehead.

Except it smells salty.

Like the waves washing onto the beach. The same as the day we rode the bike along the sand and then up onto the road.

Jem was laughing out loud. The first time since Alex had left him. I smiled with him.

Watched the gulls lifting up and up into the swollen swell of wind. Wings outstretched, gliding. So easy. Would be totally amazing. To fly free above the waves, the sand, the shore, the land.

I released my hold on Jem. Stretched out my arms.

"I'm flying," I cried. "Flying."

Jem didn't hear. His hands gripped tight around the handlebars. Strong and tanned from the summer.

The cries of the seagulls were strong. Wheeling

and diving. Breaking the skin of the sea for food.

I felt their energy. Tipped my head back to gaze at the wide sky.

We hit a rut in the sand. A narrow gully where the ocean had carved out its name.

I was jolted sideways.

"It's your own fear that is shutting him out. It's your own fear that is keeping you from him. It's what you have locked inside that is holding you back."

What's he talking about? "He wasn't in the room."

"If you say so."

Why doesn't Dark Eagle believe me?

And what do I have inside me that's keeping Jem away? I don't understand what he means.

In the first Hoodman comic all those years ago, it was hinted that Hoodman had suffered a hideous accident. Something had happened to his face. Ever since then Hoodman has kept it hidden. No one has ever seen it. Dark Eagle is his lookout. His eyes. Dark Eagle is the one who can see into the souls of men.

"First find yourself, then you will find Jem."

How can I find myself? I'm already here, aren't I? So what's he talking about? My mouth opens. Gulps like a goldfish, but no words swim out.

Aunt Chloe holds my hand, presses it against her cheek. "Come back to us, Zara."

Hey. You're as bad as Dark Eagle. I'm here. If I wasn't, you wouldn't be talking to me.

"And who on earth brought those lilies in? For goodness sake, they need to go. It makes it seem like it's a funeral in here."

I sink deep into the soft perfume she wears around her neck.

Dark Eagle's gone. He has slipped silently away, on the shadow of a wing, like he always does in the comic.

Then I hear slow and careful footsteps coming at me in the darkness.

I CURL UP SMALL. PUSH MYSELF AGAINST THE WALL AND SHUT MY EYES TIGHT. MY HEART THUDS. I DON'T WANT TO SEE. I DON'T WANT TO SEE ANYTHING.

Light leaks into my head. Leaks me back to my bedroom at home.

My room is painted green. Jem's walls are covered with nothing but posters. Bikes and birds. Not the winged birds. The ones with scraps of clothing stretched over their privates. Dad laughs at the posters, kind of enjoys them. Mom makes no comment. She probably wonders where she's gone wrong. Except she hasn't. It's just a guy thing.

On my walls are my paintings. My favorite one is of Toss, my dog who only had one eye. He got run over. He's buried between the pear tree and apple tree, down at the back of the yard. Sometimes when I feel desperate about stuff I go and talk to Toss. He always listened to me when he was alive. Dad planted a bush over him. "Breath of Heaven" it's called. Just right for a dog with one eye. I sobbed so much when it happened.

Toss and I used to go up and down the street. Him chasing me on my scooter. You'd never know he couldn't see straight. He was the bravest dog in the whole world.

That was why I drew him. I've got lots of other pictures of him. But the best one is on my wall. One day I'm getting another dog. Dad's made a promise. But so far it hasn't happened.

chapter thirteen

The footsteps have faded, gone, like they were never there.
I uncurl myself and open my eyes. Dark Eagle's wrong.
Hoodman's the guy I want to find. Not myself. If I find
Hoodman, I'll find Jem.

The truth is always dead simple once it surfaces. If Jem's
trying to find out the identity of Hoodman, then there is only
one place he'd make for and that's Hoodman's hideout.

Not that it's ever been shown in any of the comics, no
doubt to keep it secret from Morven and his evil cronies.
The drawing in the comic only ever shows one room of
Hoodman's. It could be anyone's. Just looks like a regular
place. TV, scruffy old two-seater, three chairs, none of
them matching. On the walls are two paintings. One is
of mountains in the winter. The other shows moonlight
streaming down over rolling hills.

Occasionally, they give you a clue. At the same time
they run a competition to see if anyone can guess where
Hoodman's hideout really is. Jem's nearly got there twice. He
reckons he guessed but they told him otherwise. Says it's in

the mountains or the hills. Put the paintings together, he told me, and you get the hills in front of the mountains. Jem's adamant it's in that area. In a nearby town which the pictures don't show.

So clever of him.

"Guess what, kiddo," said Jem. Using the name he'd christened me with since I was little.

"You've decided to go to college. Do a science degree."

"No way." He shook his head. Blue eyes beamed from beneath his cap.

I shrugged. "What then?"

"I reckon this time I've really sussed out where Hoodman lives."

"You yelled at me to come in for that?" I was disgusted. Jem was meant to be sorting out his future. Deciding what he was going to do when he was out of school and in the real world. It seemed like it was the last thing on his mind. "That's sure going to help you heaps next year."

"Oh that! You're getting as hyper as Mom."

"She's got a point."

"Listen," said Jem, rolling onto his back. "Mom worries about everything. It's her career."

I laughed. Couldn't help it. It was cruel, but it was the absolute truth.

"Anyway, I've decided."

"You have?" I slumped down on the end of his bed while I waited for the revelation.

"Can't you guess?"

Jem was always good at stringing me along.

"A mechanic." Thinking of his crazed love for his bike.

"Nope."

"A course at college." Then I giggled. "You're going to do drama. You've always been a bit of a drama queen."

A pillow was thrust at me. Hit me against the side of my head.

"Ha," said Jem. "Thanks for nothing."

I lay back laughing.

"What do you reckon about me working for Hoodman?"

I jerked up. Frowned. Jem was seriously losing it. "He's in a comic," I said, searching his expression to see if he was kidding.

"Yeah, yeah. I know that." He grinned and his face opened up. Taut skin over lean cheekbones like Dad, sandy-colored hair, a thin nose, and a wide generous mouth. Jem isn't good-looking. Not really. But in my book, he is nice enough. Except I've never told him that. I usually tell him he's an ugly mongrel.

"I want to get a job in the office where Hoodman's adventures are created."

"You can't draw."

"I'm not talking about that. I'm talking about an ideas man."

"Oh! An IDEAS MAN."

"Shut up. I shouldn't have told you."

"Look. It sounds great. But have you thought how it's going to happen?"

No answer.

"Besides, isn't the comic printed in the US?"

"Yeah," he acknowledged with a thoughtful nod.

"Good luck telling Mom and Dad."

Jem shrugged. "I'm going to do it, whatever it takes to be part of the team."

"You can't just walk in to a job like that."

"Why not?"

That was Jem all over. If he wanted something, he went for it. As he did with the bike. And Alex. Until she slipped through his fingers.

"Don't you dare breathe a word."

"Hardly. It's your baby."

If Jem ever got to go to the US, I can't imagine what it'd be like living without him. He belongs here. Not somewhere else. I know I am being selfish, but I've never thought about him not being around.

Just as Dark Eagle is to Hoodman. That's the way Jem is to me.

Always near the surface. Always within reach.

Most weekends Trace and I go to the mall. It's Trace's favorite place to hang out. Not so much mine. Mine is more the beach. Or the movie theater.

I absolutely love going to the movies. Anything will do. Except horror. I don't like those. Or science fiction. At best, the film has to have plenty of action plus a scene where some totally gorgeous guy saves some equally gorgeous girl. And in my imagination it is totally me.

I know it sounds stupid.

But it helps on the days when I need something to hang on to, the horrible days. When school is just too boring and things have started to creep back into my head. Started to crawl in without me noticing. Until the images flick over and over and won't leave me alone. This is when it's really, really good to get off to a film. Trace never asks why some days I'm rock bottom. She just takes me as I am. Which is what I need. Not heaps of nosy questions. I am the same with her. I don't ask about her life now or before we met. It doesn't matter. Hopefully, nothing will change now that Trace knows what happened.

But all that matters is that we're good for one another. What matters is that by some miracle she arrived at our school. My life before Trace was at a total standstill. I had a few casual friends, but none that I clicked with like Trace. It seems like she was sent especially for me.

Yeah. Yeah. Crazy head stuff.

In a way I suppose I am as bad as Jem and his comics. Believing in something that isn't true, something that doesn't make sense.

The day I went missing had been sunny with spits of warm rain. Just soft rain, sticking-out-tongue kind of rain with splotches of sunshine.

Mom was playing the piano. The tune floated out the open window into the front yard. It was mixed with the sun and raindrops, and it made them dance together. I was twirling round and round with an old pink sparkly scarf of Mom's. It was like a hoop. Round and round we went until it made me dizzy. I flopped down on the grass. The sky spun, blue and yellow and wet. Inside the house Mom was lost in the piano. When she played she seemed to get swallowed up. Dad was in the car, listening to the cricket match and Jem was inside one of his comics.

"Excuse me."

I blinked against the glare. A dark outline loomed beside our gate. The lady was wearing a big hat and dark glasses. You could hardly see any of her face at all.

"I'm looking for the Mulhollands' house."

I sat up. Stared at her as if she was stupid. How could she not know where the Mulhollands lived? Everyone knew it was the dump of a house on the corner.

"I know it's around here somewhere . . ."

"I can take you," I told her. Wanting to be important. Wanting to show her I knew more than she did.

"What about telling someone?" she said.

"I don't need to."

"Well . . . if you're sure."

I knew I wasn't allowed to get into a strange car with a strange person, but I figured it was okay to show someone to the Mulhollands' place. It was just down the street. Not far. We didn't even have to turn a corner or anything like that.

I picked up the pink sparkly scarf and tied it around my neck the same as our teacher did.

"My name's Zara," I said. "What's your name?"

"Melissa Summer," she replied.

"That's a funny last name," I told her as I skipped along.

The Melissa lady walked a bit funny. It was probably because her shoes had real high thin heels.

She smiled at me. "You're a good girl to help me like this."

chapter fourteen

I'm walking down the never-ending passageway—another one—after having turned right.

I can feel something behind me. Or someone.

"Jem. Is that you?" Knowing all the time it isn't.

Black silence slithers around me.

My stomach tightens, fearful of seeing what I don't want to see. I clench my hands into fists. Lick my dry, cracked lips.

"Trace, is that you?" I whisper.

Again nothing.

Hairs on my neck prick. Sweat beads my forehead.

I cling to what little courage I have left.

Then turn.

There is nothing. Nobody.

My whole body sags to the ground. I rock back and forth. Clench my arms around my knees. Make myself as small as I can. That way no one will see me. I've had it. I'll just stay like this until I can figure out what's going on.

The corridor crouches around me.

Out of the corner of my eye I see the wall move.

A LONG, WIDE CRACK APPEARS.

I JERK AWAY IN HORROR.

THERE INSIDE THE CRACK IS THE LARGEST LIZARD I'VE EVER SEEN.

Eyes glittering, gazing right at me as if it wants to devour me. Its sharp claws stretching, flexing. The crack widens. Chunks of the wall fall away, thud to the ground.

I need to move. Get away from here.

Exhaustion drags at my heels.

I stagger off. Close your mind to any thoughts, I tell myself. Just get away from the creature.

The pain in my leg throbs. The constant ache won't let me alone. It's not there, I tell myself. It's not there. Like in the end *he* wasn't there. Even when his fingers were touching my hair, they weren't there. Him with those big watery eyes, the same as the Melissa lady, slobbery lips and funny smell. Not allowed to tell. Mustn't ever tell.

Now I'm running.

There's no pain. There's nothing to feel. Not in my head, or my legs or arms.

I'm getting away, just as I did that day on the beach with Trace and the high heels. And when I escaped from that other place. It's like all of it is trapped inside me. Shoved down into a deep pit since the afternoon when Melissa Summer took my hand and we walked down the street together toward the Mulhollands' house on the corner.

The thing still waits, ready to pounce. Leap out of its scared hidey-hole. Grab at me again.

On and on down the long corridor I travel. A race that's

going nowhere, except away from the creature.

My legs give way. I stumble. Clutch at air. Lurch at the wall. Slam into it with my shoulder and the side of my head. I'm breaking into little pieces. Bit by bit I'm being hammered into tiny fragments. As if I'm the shell path: from shards to splinters to dust.

Broken.

I hear the lizard. Heavy lumbering. Close behind with its clumsy footsteps.

It can't get me. Mustn't. What will happen to Jem if it did? He'd be stuck in the comic forever.

The corridor shakes, rumbles.

Or is it the sound inside my head?

I'm not sure. Not sure of anything anymore.

I'm totally exhausted. All I want is to curl up at the end of Jem's bed and talk to him. As I've always done. Half the time Jem never really listened, but he pretended different. Trace reckoned it was a bit odd. Me confiding in Jem about everything. She said it wasn't natural.

"And your family is?" I had replied.

As soon as I said that, I wanted the words back. They were mean and not fair. No way was her family her fault.

Trace said nothing. She shrugged and walked off.

It was three days before she let me into her space again.

I apologized a hundred times. She didn't. Not once. So after that I never talked about Jem and me again. How I've always needed him. How if things hadn't happened, then maybe it might have been different. Maybe we'd have fought more and gone our own way. But I needed Jem. As Jem needed Hoodman.

I pull away from the wall.

I'm half a whole.

I need to keep moving.

I put one foot in front of the other. They sink down into a white space, as if the comic's illustrator hasn't had time to catch up with me and where I am. Hasn't had time to draw anything else on the page except me trying to escape the creature.

I have to get away.

The night I fled from the cupboard house, I ran along the wet pavement with no shoes, my feet making a whimpering, terrified sound, little sobs escaping from my throat and the scarf clutched tight in my hand. The lovely, pink sparkly scarf. I still have it. It's the one bit that is the same.

Running as fast as I could, I sucked in the dark trees, the warm wind, and the quiet houses. I pulled them all into me. Right into my center so they couldn't escape.

Now it's the lizard after me. Not far behind. With heavy breathing and footsteps.

I need to wipe him out with my eraser. But how can I? If I pause, he'll have me. Drag me back into the wall, hide me in the crack so no one will ever find me. Just got to keep moving.

Lots of times after I was back home again I liked to be with Dad. Mostly, I knew where to find him, but sometimes I didn't.

"Dad. Where are you?"

Then I heard the radio and knew.

I walked down the side path to the front of our house.

Dad was sitting in the car listening to the cricket match. He often did that. Mom wasn't the slightest bit interested in sports, so he got out of her way when the match was on to keep her happy.

"What's up?"

"I don't want to go anymore."

Dad raised his eyebrows. He knew what I was talking about without asking.

"It's stupid," I told him through the open window. "The doctor man keeps asking me the same questions over and over."

Dad turned down the radio. Opened the door. I slipped into the front seat beside him.

"Okay. I'll talk to Mom. See what she says."

I pulled a face. "She'll say it's for my own good. But I'm okay."

Dad ruffled my hair. "I agree, the whole thing seems to be a bit of a no-brainer."

We sat together in silence. It was cozy in the car. Nothing could ever get to you in there. You knew you were always going to be safe.

"You know Mom's busy organizing a surprise birthday for you," said Dad with a wicked smile. "I shouldn't be telling, but . . ."

His voice faltered. I knew he told me out of comfort.

"Eight years old. You're growing up far too fast, young lady."

I grinned. "I know about the party. Stupid Lillian

Russell let it out by mistake. She asked me what I wanted for a present."

Dad laughed. It was a warm laugh. Not over the top. It made you want to stay close. "You want to listen to the match with me?"

"Yeah. Okay."

It was nice being with Dad in the car. Just the two of us. With the rest of the world locked out.

It was one of my all-time favorite places.

chapter fifteen

"Who did this drawing?"

I put up my hand.

My teacher nodded. She had a crooked mouth which looked like a rubber band that had busted.

That was what I had drawn. Her and that mouth. I know her mouth was ugly, so that's how I drew it.

"I think we need to have a little talk, Zara. Please remain behind after class."

So I did.

"You have deliberately made me look like some sort of monster. You can't go round drawing people in that way. It's very hurtful," she said when the classroom was all quiet and there was only her and me and my drawing.

I didn't answer.

"Plus I'm not sure you even drew it."

"Yes, I did."

"Hmmm."

"You're sure your brother didn't do it?"

I gaped at her with surprise. "He can't draw for anything."

Mrs. Reid pulled her mouth. Her lips looked like they were going to snap.

I tried not to giggle. "I think I got the nose a bit wrong."

"Are you being smart?"

"No," I said, shaking my head.

Later on, Mom said, "Perhaps, it'd be better if you didn't draw teachers."

"I wanted to draw her mouth. It's different than other mouths."

Dad chortled.

"She wanted to know if you'd done it," I said to Jem. "I told her you couldn't draw for nuts."

"Where is the drawing?" asked Dad. His brown eyes smiling at me. I knew I was his favorite.

"Mrs. Reid has it," I told them.

"Only three years at school and she's already in trouble," said Jem, his expression one of teasing.

I did the drawing one night in bed. I was bored so I got out my pad and Mrs. Reid's face just arrived in my head. I got it down on the paper fast. When I'd finished I was really pleased with it. It was the first time I'd drawn a face.

I thought she'd be pleased that I drew her. Even though it made her mouth look horrible.

"How are you doing, Mr. Wilson?"

"Okay, thanks."

"And Mrs. Wilson?"

"We both have our moments."

"Yes, I'm sure. From what I've been told, Zara's got a strong will."

Dad sighs. "She doesn't seem to be responding to anything. Sometimes I wonder where Zara really is."

"Give her time."

That's silly. There is no time.

All that matters is getting away from this creature, with its smelly breath. Getting away from its consuming hunger for me.

Where's Dark Eagle when I need him?

And Hoodman?

And Jem?

"Someone help me," I cry. But no one hears. No one sees me. I'm stuck in a corridor without any end.

Stuck in a small locked cupboard.

Who's crying? I don't know. I can't see; it's too dark in here. There's no space to breathe.

He used to watch me from the outside. I know he did. I could feel him. Behind the blindfold, I imagined his eye flicking over the small hole in the door.

THE LIZARD SNAPS. CATCHES MY HEEL. I GO DOWN. SMASH AGAINST THE GROUND.

FEEL ITS TEETH DIG DEEP, RIP AT MY LEG.

My mouth feels as if it is full of gravel or sand. I spit. Small bright droplets of blood splatter into the air.

The blood is like the lights of the houses.

Don't stop. The man is coming after me. Hunting me down.

Thud, thud.

Run, Zara.

Where is everyone?

Where is my home?

"Hey, girl. It's me checking in again to see if you're still lying around doing nothing. Might have known. For God's sake. You need to get a grip. Hey! How about this? You like it? Thought you would. Got it at the marketplace on Sunday. Yeah. Yeah. I know. Not a good place to be seen in. But you really should see the stuff this one girl has. Makes all the jewelry herself. Such totally cool gear. Was going to buy you a necklace, but couldn't decide, so you'll have to come with me."

Small sounds come and go as Trace yaks on. The swish of a curtain. Quiet steps. A cough. I've forgotten where I am. It seems like no place I know. Or have been to before. Or what I'm doing here.

"Good. You agree. The market's a promise. My treat. So no worries there. And guess what? You don't feel like guessing. Okay. I'll tell you. Saw Paul yesterday."

I jolt. At the mention of Paul, my heart quickens.

"Thought that'd get your attention. Him and that shark bitch Chelsea are no longer together. He dumped her after you and Jem . . ."

Silence.

Me and Jem what? Tell me. Don't stop.

"This is such shit. I can't do it any longer." Trace's words gulp as if she wants them back.

Trace. Me and Jem what?

My question lies unanswered.

"Hey! I've brought you this. It's just a loan, mind you. Thought you might like to use it."

I smell her face full of white and dark makeup. She places the small soft buds of her iPod into my ears.

I like it. I've been after one for ages. I don't ask if it's fallen off the back of a truck.

Music flows through my head, through my blood. Tears fill my eyes. It's like I've come home.

"You just have to press here to turn it on and then here to turn it off. If you can't do it someone will, you just . . ."

Trace's voice gets smaller and smaller.

I'm lying face down in the corridor. I lick at the blood on my lips. It's sticky. I lift my head. Turn slowly. Turn away from the continual dull ache in my shoulder.

The corridor is empty. The lizard creature has vanished. Or is it hiding? Has it somehow made itself invisible?

Not waiting to find out, I haul myself up.

The corridor is the same. White and soundless. The inside of a tube, as if I've been swallowed by a pale worm. At least there are no blue doors.

I walk. Take one step. Two steps. I'm totally stiff. I was never like this after the sprints at school. I need to work out more. Go to the gym. I will again. Except this time Paul won't be there. He'll avoid the gym at all costs. At least that's what I'm guessing.

Stupid, stupid me. Trying to be smart. Not realizing how much he really did care. But I find it hard to trust.

Now, where the hell is Jem? I never thought it'd be this difficult to find him.

I'm getting sick of all this. What happened to the plan of finding him and getting us out and back home?

My plan's hit a wall. Nothing is working out the way it was meant to.

Okay. Then it's time to make stuff happen. No more mucking about.

I pull out my pencil. Step up to the wall. Close my eyes

and visualize the comic again. See the picture of Hoodman's room.

I work fast. The sketch takes shape. There are the chairs, the sofa. I've got to get it right. Otherwise who knows where I'll end up.

What else did the comic show?

The paintings. One had mountains, the other moonlight on the hills.

Is there anything else?

I try to relax, pretend I'm looking at the comic over Jem's shoulder. Hey. That's right. There was a TV sitting in the corner. Crazy to think of Hoodman with a TV, the great unknown who saves the world from disasters watching the news. Funny, really. Suppose they wanted to make it look like he had a bit of a normal life. The TV had something on top of it. What? Think, Zara. See it in your mind.

It was a figure of some description. I wish I'd paid more attention. An animal. No. A bird. My mind stills. Yeah. That's it. A bird. Then I laugh out loud. Of course. Dummy. An eagle. Dark Eagle.

I sketch in the TV and the eagle. Then I stand back and gaze at my masterpiece. Except it isn't. It's rough as anything. But it'll have to do.

Okay. Now all it needs is a border. A bold black line around the edge to contain the room.

As I draw it in, I smell ink, the kind that I imagine newspapers use.

Once I've finished, I suck in a long breath and thrust my foot at the wall. It plunges deep into the picture.

A great whooshing sound fills my ears. Roars through my head. It's like I'm being sucked into a vacuum. I'm out of control, flying, and then falling fast. Dropping down into a deep and wide darkness.

"She's alive."

I feel a great thumping on my chest.

Thump, thump.

Don't. It hurts.

"Ambulance is taking its time."

Take away the light. It's too bright. It's burning my eyes to pieces.

"Easy. Easy with the bike. God! What a mess!"

And the noise. Stop it. Stop the screaming siren sound.

I clamp my hands over my ears.

I am swept into a black and long silence. A place that is peaceful.

A place where nothing can hurt me.

chapter sixteen

The room smelled as if it had been stuffed in a drawer too long.

"Let's sit over here," whispered Mom.

We went over to the chairs near a fish tank. I sat and watched the fish. The ones I liked the best were yellow, orange, and shiny. They flicked around in the water. They stared at me with their glass eyes. I didn't like that. I looked away.

Mom pretended to read a magazine. I gazed at the wall. It was a boring wall. There was nothing on it.

Down the corridor I heard the quiet click of a door. A skinny man appeared in front of us. He had sticking-out hair, glasses, and a tall face. It appeared stretched out, as if it had been made from gum. His thin nose and mouth seemed like they had been glued on. He smiled at us.

"Mrs. Wilson."

Mom nodded.

"And Zara," he added. Like I had been tacked

on to Mom. But we had come here for me, so that wasn't right.

Mom put down the magazine and we followed the man and his quick springy steps.

We went into a small room where a desk took up most of it. The top was heaped up with folders and papers. He seemed more like a teacher. But I knew he wasn't.

"A psychologist," Mom had told me. "That's who we're going to see."

"Why?"

"Because of what happened."

"What's he do?"

"He helps people."

"How does he help them?"

Mom had sighed. Her eyes were pinched and sad. "He helps sort out things."

The man held out his hand to Mom. "Dr. Beardsley," he said, watching me. But pretending not to. But I could tell. You had to be quick to notice stuff like that, and I saw it.

"And you must be Zara."

I nodded.

"Good."

What was so good about me nodding?

We sat down. The psychologist man was silent for a bit. Then he leaned forward. "Zara, I hear you're very good at drawing," he said in a dribbly sort of voice.

I nodded again.

"While I talk to your mother I'd like you to draw something for me."

"Anything at all?" I was staring at his hair when I said this because it looked like a good thing to draw.

"Yes. Anything you want."

He gave me several pieces of paper. "I have some crayons. Or a pencil if you would prefer?"

"Crayons are for babies. A pencil's better. And some pens if you've got them."

He rummaged around another drawer. Handed over a packet of felt pens. They had thin tips. I liked the ones that weren't so thin, but I guessed that those would have to do.

I thought hard. Then I knew what I wanted to draw. My bedroom at home. I drew my bed with its pink cover with rainy-blue sploshes. Least that was what they looked like to me. Beside my bed was a white table with two drawers. On the top was a light, except it didn't work anymore. I'd had it for a long time before it got busted. My friend Jessie and

I were playing and it got knocked off. Over at the side wall, along from the door, was a white cupboard with lots of drawers. They had silver knobs. I drew them in carefully. That was because they were really, really pretty. Flowers with a star inside. Then I put in the door. I left it half open because that way I could hear Mom and Dad talking and the sound of the TV. Those were nice sounds to hear. I looked at my drawing. Next I put in the wardrobe. That door was closed so you couldn't see all the mess stuffed into the bottom. It was meant to be neat and tidy, but it couldn't be helped. There was nowhere else to put my toys. Dad kept saying when the garage was finished the overflow of my stuff could go in there, but Mom knew that was probably never going to happen. She didn't get enough money working at the supermarket and Dad had a bad back. But at least he was able to serve customers behind the counter at the local gas station. He said he enjoyed it. Meeting the different people. Dad has got to know heaps and he's popular as well. But even with both jobs it didn't give them enough money to complete the garage. I said I would save up for it with my pocket money. Jem had laughed and teased me by saying, what pocket money?

"Finished, Zara?"

The voice climbed into my head. Where did it come from? Anyway I hadn't finished. I was still busy with my room. On the wall just along from my bed was a small window. That particular window looked down onto a brown fence. It was where cranky old Ken lived. That's what Dad called him. So did I, because he never said hello or anything nice to anyone. The other window on the other side of the room was bigger and much nicer. From there I could see the front yard, with its gardens and trees and grass.

"Zara," said Mom. "Dr. Beardsley is waiting."

I glanced up. I was snapped out of my bedroom and whooshed back into the small room with the man with the tall face and sticking-out hair.

"You've been very busy," he said.

"You told me to do a drawing. I've been doing what you said."

"Do you always do what you're told?"

I shrugged. "Sometimes." He stared at me through his glasses. His eyes looked like the fish in the tank. And like the one eye through the hole in the cupboard.

"May I have a look?"

"It's not finished. I don't like people to see my drawings before they're finished."

"Just a quick peek."

I shook my head.

Mom smiled at me. "I'd love to see it."

"Just you then. Not him."

Mom lifted up the drawing. "It's your bedroom. It's very good. Couldn't I show Dr. Beardsley?"

"In a minute," I said, taking the picture back.

I went back to the drawing and drew in the other window and then scribbled over the glass all black. Then I handed it over.

Dr. Beardsley looked at my picture. His hand rubbed his chin. Perhaps he was feeling for spots.

"This is your bedroom at home?"

"Yes."

"You are quite an artist." His finger pointed to the windows. "You've colored in the glass."

"It's dark outside," I said. Anyone would know that. He wasn't very smart if he didn't even know that.

"Can we go now?" I asked Mom.

Mom turned to me. Glints of wetness rimmed the edges of her eyes. She didn't need to cry any more. I had already told her a hundred-million times I was okay.

chapter seventeen

It's weird. Being in Hoodman's lounge.

It's his place all right and not just my drawing of it. There are things here that I never drew. There are the cushions on the sofa. Three of them with patterns like a crossword.

There's nobody in the room. Only me.

Now what?

"Jem," I call.

No reply.

Even with the stuff in the room it feels empty. It's just like a picture in the comic. I laugh as I imagine someone in a shop picking up the comic, flicking through it and seeing me sneaking through Hoodman's lounge. How great would that be?

Trace would love it. It's the kind of thing she dreams of happening.

"Can't stand this place."

"What place?" Trace and I were sitting in the mall, our backs to the fountain. Water splashed over the edges of a naked nymph's shoulders. Sun spilled through the trees growing out of the paved ground. "You mean here? This place. You want to move? Go somewhere else?"

Trace shook her head. Her black eyelids shut out her eyes. "Sometimes, Zara, you're doomed."

I laughed. "Yeah. Yeah. You too."

"Ha! I'm out of this place as soon as I can."

"You mean the town?"

"What else. It's so nothing, man." She ripped open her bag of onion chips. Bit into one. Fragments exploded. "What's here? Nothing. The guys are dopey. Clubbing's hardly been heard of. The shops are deader than dead."

I listened and listened. Trace had been there before. It was always about getting out, getting away. I had no idea what she thought lay out there. But I knew better than to argue. I knew her obsession with "getting the hell out of it" would pass in a bit and she'd be back to sourcing out what was on offer again.

"Stuff it," she exclaimed. "Don't look."

"What? Why?"

Then I saw them. Paul and Chelsea. She was hanging on to him like he was made of glue.

My heart thudded. It was loud in my ears. My heart felt as if it was banging all over the place. I stared at the ground as they neared. I wanted to see him gazing at me, and feel his eyes on me. Feel them caressing my skin, feel that heat pass between our lips. But I had gone and ruined it well and truly.

"You want me to mess her up?" said Trace when they'd gone into the department store.

I know it was her way of giving me comfort. She'd never do such a thing, but for a moment I wanted to scream out yes, yes, go and mess her up good.

"Come on. Like you said, it's time to get out of here."

Curtains cover the one window. I know Hoodman doesn't like light. I go over and pull them across. Outside it's pitch black. I peer through the darkness, trying to see the lights of the city. There are none. That's strange. There are always lights. Ones from other buildings, the streetlights, car lights. It doesn't make any sense unless there's been a power outage, but then the light in here wouldn't be on. I step away from the window. It feels too creepy for words.

With a shiver I wrap my arms around myself, trying to ward off the chill that has sneaked around me. At least I'm not in the corridor any longer. I'm away from Morven.

But this isn't finding Jem.

I need to get him home. And me. The two of us. Then everything will be okay.

"Jem," I cry out.

Come on. Where are you? I felt for sure you'd be here, in Hoodman's hideout.

I'm sick of this. Tired. I need to rest. My head is sore. It aches constantly. All I hear are strange sounds clawing to get out. Why can't I make them stop?

Tears stick to the inside of my lashes. I blink. Swallow the pity.

THUMP.
MY FOOT LANDS ON IT. SQUASHES IT. POUNDS IT INTO THE FLOOR.

Are Morven and his squad close by? Have they got lookouts everywhere? Even in Hoodman's place?

Next moment I hear the sound of water.

What the . . . ?

I hold my breath and listen.

There it is again.

It's coming from the wall.

I strain to hear. Strain to see.

Blink.

There in the picture with the mountains is a river. It wasn't there before. I swear.

I step closer and see wetness seeping from the frame and dripping onto the floor.

"She's wet the bed again," said Mom.

I felt myself lifted up and my pajamas stripped. Shivery cold, I clung to my sleep. New clean pajamas were pulled on. Dry. Cuddly. I sank back into my bed, my nice safe bedroom. Back to sleep.

I see Jem's cap. It's in the river. I go closer. Step in the puddle. What's he doing in the picture? I must be seeing things. Imagining things. But what if it really is his cap? Then I need it. My fingers go toward the picture, the river, and the cap. The water is freezing. I catch hold of the tiny red speck. Pull it out of the painting. It grows in my hand.

It's Jem's. No doubt about it. There's the Astro scrawled across the front. I feel sick, a burning in my throat. Has he drowned? No—he can't have. Jem is too smart for that.

"Jem," I scream. His name ripping across my lips. "Where are you?"

"I saw her lips twitch. I know I did. What are you trying to tell us, Zara?"

Mom, is that you? Where are you?

"Talk to me. I'm here. Right by your side."

You are not. Why's she lying to me? Mom hates fibs. Even the small white ones.

There's no one here except me.

Not Hoodman, Dark Eagle, or Jem.

I sink down to my knees.

"Go away," I scream at the siren in my head. "Just go away and leave me alone."

chapter eighteen

Paul's brown hair hangs straight, lies long over part of his forehead. His black eyebrows are the same as his eyes: dark, dark. Looking into them, you're in a deep place. He has an easy walk. Long relaxed steps, loping. I like that in a guy. First time I noticed him, he was walking, slow-like, with his mates. He caught my eye but I pretended I hadn't seen him.

That night sitting up in bed I drew him. The exact moment when he had focused on me. I tried to capture that on the page. It wasn't a glance; it was much more than that. Since then I've done heaps more drawings of him. But none like that original one with his first fleeting look. I knew then, like he did, that we'd get together. As if somewhere it had already been planned. Drawn out in a grid that exactly at so-and-so time, on so-and-so day and year we would be within smiling distance of one another. Sounds totally stupid I know, but I can't explain it any better than that.

I loved the smell of him. His drops of sweat. I felt his smell belonged to me and that it was all mine.

We often went to the beach. The shell one that gave our home the white path.

One particular time when Paul's arm was draped loose around my shoulders I felt like crying. Just putting my head on his chest and weeping. Telling him about the thing that had happened to me. It was crazy. I'd never felt like that before with anyone. Not that I've had many boyfriends. Two in fact. One when I was eleven, William Brooks who had ginger hair and freckles, and the next one not long after I was twelve. Julian Ross. He was into cricket. Dad liked him. Thought he was great. Eventually, Julian drifted off, saying I was a bit too weird for him. That's been it. Not a long line of love affairs. Just two guys who were okay, nothing more. There were others who found *me* okay, like Brian Hamlock now, who I never encouraged.

But with Paul I knew right off it was going to be different. Then I went and did that utterly stupid thing with Jack. It was probably because we were getting too close. It's never been my thing to get that close to anyone. It's something in my makeup.

Like that doctor psychologist man. The way he kept on and on asking me the same questions, it was horrible. Always putting them to me in different ways. Wanting to catch me out. As if I wouldn't notice. Even back then when I was seven, I knew. He kept trying to get me to tell him if I knew who had taken me. Where I'd been kept.

"Didn't you tell the police it was a woman?"

"I suppose so."

"So you saw her?"

I nodded. The psychologist person was silly. He never asked if there was anyone else, so he was never going to know about the man and I was glad, because it kept me safe.

"Could you tell me about her?"

Mustn't tell.

I was hiding. Sitting in his office I was hiding with my mouth shut.

"Zara, no one's going to harm you if you tell the truth."

I hated that room. I didn't want to come anymore.

Silence. Neither of us spoke. I scowled at the floor. I wasn't coming next week. I wasn't.

Mom didn't come in with me now. She hadn't for

the last few times. She used to. Then she said I was able to go by myself. She waited in the coffee shop downstairs. I know that the doctor man told her not to come.

He wrote something down on his big white pad.

"What sort of things did she say to you?"

I stayed hidden in the chair. It wasn't her. It was him. He only said words in whispers. Ones that got right into my head. Where they stayed for weeks and months and were still there. Hiding down that dark hole. When I lay in bed after I was back and everyone was asleep, the voice was there, whispering all sorts of things. Telling me I was his pet. Telling me he'd look after me for always. And that he had been waiting for someone like me for a very long time and that he had always wanted a doll, but now he had me instead.

"Where did she touch you?"

"Nowhere." I was out of my hiding place. I wanted to yell at him. But I didn't. If I did, he'd keep on and on at me. So I spoke quietly instead. "She liked my hair a lot."

"Why do you think she took you?"

I shrugged and folded my arms.

"Can you draw me a picture of where you were?"

I'd already drawn it a hundred times. But it was

better than answering all his stupid questions.

He gave me a piece of paper and a pencil.

"And you weren't frightened at all?"

I shook my head. It was a lie. A whopper.

The only person I told the truth to was Jem.

But first I made him cross his heart and say out loud that he hoped to die if he told Mom or Dad. Or anyone else.

"Cross my heart," he said with that wide grin of his, "and hope to die if I tell."

After I finished telling him everything, about how strange it was that Melissa Summer and the man had kind of the same voice, except Melissa's was a bit more squeaky than the man's and how they had the same damp, slimy hands and how I didn't wear the blindfold in the cupboard when I was on my own, but when I heard him coming I shoved it back on, because he'd told me I had to do that as soon as I heard him coming. Or else. It was the way he said "or else" that frightened me the most. I didn't want to see him anyway. He always made sure my eyes were covered before he took me to the toilet or sat me on his knee and sang to me, or gave me something to eat and drink. I told Jem that the Melissa lady must have been too busy to come so she sent her brother instead.

Jem didn't tell me that I should let the psychologist man know everything I'd told him. Or Mom or Dad.

The only thing Jem said was that he thought the man and the woman were probably the same person, and that some men liked to dress up as women, to which I had opened my mouth like a goldfish trying to gulp in some air.

I don't know how Jem knew about that. Especially, when he was only ten years old. He said he'd heard about it at school.

And then when I told him how I was locked inside a cupboard and how small it was and dark and about the peephole where I knew the man's eye stared in at me and when he wasn't there how the only thing left was a bright blue door, Jem's eyes filled with tears and he couldn't look at me.

chapter nineteen

I STUFF JEM'S CAP IN MY POCKET. IT DOESN'T MATTER THAT IT'S WET.

THEN I STARE AT THE PAINTING. THE RIVER HAS STOPPED DRIPPING ONTO THE FLOOR.

I squint at it long and hard. My brother's not there. I'm sure of it. But what makes me so certain? I shrug. I don't know; it's just a feeling. The only thing I know for real is that Jem goes nowhere without his cap.

I stand there feeling worn out and lost. I want to sit down and weep, but it's too late for all that, I need to keep going so I pull back my shoulders.

"You're not going to win," I shout. "I don't care how long it takes. You're not keeping Jem. He's coming home with me. You understand?"

My throat cracks. Why is it so quiet? What happened to my words? I said them. I know I did. But I didn't hear them. They left my lips without making a sound.

It feels as if I'm going crazy.

Got to get out of here.

I can't use the window—it's way too high from the ground.

And there's no door.

I take my pencil and scribble all over Hoodman's room. Scribble and scribble until it is all covered up.

"Hey, girl. You and me are crazy," cried Trace, threading her arm through mine, taking off. Running down the street, dodging anyone in our way. The two of us laughing, my stomach aching from it.

The last day of term.

Free. Out of it. Away from those mean, tight walls. The endless homework. What was it all for anyway? I was going to be an artist, so what was the use of all the studying? Trace reckoned she was going to be a nothing. But an Important Nothing.

Or, if she really, really had to be something, she was going to be a Shopping Mall Junkie.

She skittered to a halt outside the entrance to Broad Street.

"What?" I asked her.

She turned and pouted. Her Goth face a stand-off. "Got to get home."

I didn't ask why. I did once and was told to mind my own business. "Ten minutes," I said. "A celebration. A double-chocolate smoothie. My treat."

The pout was gone. We were off again. Through the doors and into the grand entrance, under the massive glass dome, past the fountain, the plastic palms, until we were sucked up into the piped music like pulling a milkshake through a straw.

My hands were wrapped around my knees while my eyes tried not to look at the small round peephole. I was shivering with fright. The pink sparkly scarf a ball in my scared hands. Jem would come soon and get me. And Mom and Dad. They'd know where I was. Where to find me. I lifted my foot and kicked at the door. It juddered. I did it again and again. Silence swallowed up my useless kicking. My eyes

filled with sticky tears. Above my fright I heard a
sound. It was a door opening. Carefully. Quietly,
I heard soft footsteps. I sucked back my tears.
Mustn't let him see me cry. Mustn't show him
I'm afraid.

"Are your eyes covered?" came the far-off
whisper. "Cover your eyes."

I felt for the piece of rag on the floor. Pulled it
over my head. My eyes disappeared.

"Tell me. Are you ready?"

I nodded.

"Tell me," he breathed.

"I'm ready."

"Good. You know what happens if you aren't.
Don't you? If you lie."

"Yes. I know."

Footsteps came into the room, then a click.

The cupboard door opened. The funny smell was
there. Damp. Slobbery. I pushed myself into the
corner.

His hands found me. "Time to pee."

"Hey, girl," comes the voice of Trace, *"there's someone to
see you."*

Go away. Leave me alone. I don't want to

see anyone. Except Jem. You're taking away my concentration. Don't you understand? This is a matter of life and death.

"Say something, Marsha."

"Hi, Zara."

What! Not Marsha Henshaw. What's Trace doing with a loser like her? Last time Marsha tried to crash our twosome Trace told her where to go. Why's she hanging out with her all of a sudden?

I don't get it.

"Talk to her."

Why does Marsha need to talk to me? What's she done?

"Hi, Zara."

"You've said that. Jeez. What a bird brain. How about saying something different?"

"I don't know what else to say. It's a bit hard when she doesn't answer you back."

"Yeah . . . well . . . make an effort. Pretend Zara's sitting up and looking at you like I do. Go on try it and say something."

"It's raining outside."

"It'd hardly be raining inside," says Trace, her voice full of sharp barbs. *"I didn't realize you were so thick."*

"I didn't have to come . . ."

I drift while they're arguing.

Jem was doubling me on his bike. He said when
he got a new two-wheeler he was going to give
the old one to me. I was nine and he was twelve.
The bike had a buckled wheel and the handlebars
were mangled. He and Dad got it from the dump.
Jem told me it was just lying there waiting for
him. He smuggled it into his bedroom. It would
have been better, he said, if we'd had a garage,
but we didn't. When Mom saw the crusty old
bike lying next to Jem's bed she went and told
Dad off, not Jem.

Jem fixed up the bike. Kind of. It took weeks.
Then one day he wheeled it outside and hopped on.
He rode it round and round the yard grinning his
eyeballs off. Even Mom said he'd done a great job.
Dad just nodded and smiled. His smile casual and
warm, kind of like it was leaning on his face.

That was when I got to have my first bike double.

Off we went, down the street. Wobbling a bit.
Giggling and laughing a lot.

I tipped my head back, way back, while hanging
on to the handlebars. I saw the sun winking at me

through the trees and felt the light wind brush through my hair.

"Did you know that Ryan and me are in the pop idol contest at school?" says Marsha.

"Listen, moron. How could she know?" This hiss comes from Trace.

Marsha ignores the comment. "We're pretty good, even if I do say so myself."

Trace laughs. "Like a pop idol is for two."

"Mr. Barnett's thinking about it."

"Whenever has Mr. Barnett ever thought about anything?"

"You think you're always right. Don't you?" says Marsha. "Well, this time you watch. You're going to be sooooo wrong."

"Yeah, right," says Trace. "The same as your singing partner, Ryan? You really have to be sick. He can't sing. Not a note. And the pop idol song contest is for one. Dummy."

"At least," retaliates Marsha, "he's giving it a go. Which is more than you're doing."

Trace sniffs. "I'd win it if I entered. It's as simple as that."

"What!"

It's good to hear the banter. Even though most of it's meaningless.

"Isn't that right, Zara?"

Totally.

"Only if they were auditioning for cackling hens."
Marsha snorts with raucous laughter.

chapter twenty

There's something here with me in this moist, sticky darkness. I can't see what. But I know there is.

"Dark Eagle, is that you?" It has to be. It's what he does in the comic. He's there, but he isn't. You get to see the tip of a wing, a claw on the ground, the gleam of an eye, a wing shadow and you know it's him.

No answer.

Just a stagnant stillness.

I stare into the blackness I created. Gaze hard into it. The more my eyes focus, the more it looks like a giant railway. Lines traveling over lines. The way the pencil slashed across the room, a mesh of anger.

I feel a sly movement to the side of me.

I jump. Push myself away. Everything feels slimy. I need to see what's here with me. It could be hundreds of scorpions for all I know. I rub at the hidden room with my eraser until a splinter of light spears the black. I rub some more. Now I have a spool of light.

It's a hole big enough for me to escape through.

I lie flat and wiggle. It feels like a burrow. The same as my bed on cold nights when I make myself a funnel and slip down into it, leaving only my nose out. The same as the burrow I made for myself in the cupboard. Right up against the left corner. A spider in a web. But he always found me.

THE DAILY TIMES

BIG TURNOUT FOR ACCIDENT VICTIM

The funeral for Jem Wilson, who died as a result of a motorcycle accident four days ago while swerving to avoid a toddler, was today held at Seaview Church. It was a moving service with many of the pupils and teachers from Riverstone High attending. More than twenty students gave testimony to his being "a real decent guy in all respects."

The family of Marie Suri paid tribute to the actions shown by the deceased.

The Wilson family were all in attendance, except for his sister, Zara, who still remains in a coma.

chapter twenty-one

"Hello, sweetie. How you doing today?"

Fine.

"Barry says to say hi."

Aunt Chloe's partner. He came into her life one
day about three years ago. Just when she was getting
desperate, according to Mom. Chloe married
young and divorced young. Her own fault, says
Mom, more than once. Since then Chloe has built
up a career in advertising. Now she runs her own
business. Barry's into real estate.

*"I've just seen Trace. You've got a loyal friend there. We
were all wrong about her it seems."*

Yeah, I think. You were. A breeze drifts over my
face. I smell the warmth. Smell the turning trees, the
lost leaves, the worn-out grass, and the brimming
armful of sunshine.

*"Better shut the window before it blows everything all over
the place."*

No, I shout. Leave it open. I like the air. I need it.

Please.

The window snaps shut.

"Anyway, girl, here's what's happening. The pop idol starts tomorrow. Sixty kids on the list. Sixty. All of them hoping like hell they're going to be the winner. You gotta feel sorry for the judges. Oh yeah! And guess who they are? You can't? Okay. First off there's Mr. Barnett. He's the chief slouch. What's he know about pop idols at his age? I ask you. A big fat nothing, I reckon."

I couldn't agree more.

"Next we have Ms. Fran Winter. Give us a break. She knows stuff all about math; so what's her pop idol credential? Suppose it's because she's young and might recognize something from the pop world. Last is farty old Baked Beans."

Baked Beans got his name because he always lets one off in class. We haven't had him as a teacher. Next year maybe. Can't wait. Ha-ha.

Trace laughs. "He'll probably clear the hall before the competition even gets started."

What about Marsha and Ryan?

"And," goes on Trace, "in case you're wondering about the duo idol of Marsha and Ryan—that's been canceled. Given the chop. Last time I saw Marsha she was grinding

her teeth and swearing at Mr. Barnett's back. And giving him the finger. Also seen by Hector, our darling second-in-command, principal of vice. She vanished into his office and hasn't been talking much since. She's totally thick. Thinking duo for the contest. Going double in a singles bar. Ha-ha. Get it?"

I get it. I get it. I need to sleep.

"Hello, Trace."

"Hi."

"Any change?"

"Not that I can see. I'd better get moving."

"Thanks," says Mom. *"I know Zara loves having you here."*

"Yeah. Well."

Soft footsteps.

See you, Trace.

I feel an arm slide around my shoulders. Mom's arm. The feeling is nice. I want to snuggle into it forever.

Where was everyone? Where was our house?

The pale streetlight spluttered at me. I heard a noise. A car, going slow. It was crawling along the street behind me.

Bushes whacked my face. I crumpled down. Down

onto the damp earth. Shaking, shivering, wetting my underwear, warm pee trickling down my leg. He wasn't allowed to find me. No one was allowed to see me. I clutched at the scarf. Pressed it to my chest. Make me disappear. Make me not here. Make me not anywhere.

The car slid by.

"Come on. Please," I said to Jem. "I'm bored."

Jem didn't reply. He just rustled his comic, pretending I wasn't there.

I stood right by him and sighed twice.

"Zara."

"Just one ride. Where's the harm?"

Jem lowered the comic until his eyes were visible. "It'll cost you," he said with a grin.

"I'm not paying."

"Then too bad. No ride. No wind rushing through your hair. No speed throbbing through . . ." The comic went back up, blocking his face.

What Jem said was true. I loved being on the back of the Triumph. It was like once we were on the road, something happened. I just wanted to go faster and faster.

"What do you want?"

"What's it worth?"

"Oh, come on, Jem. Stop teasing."

The comic was dropped beside him. He pushed himself up against the bed end. "Draw her."

"You mean draw the bike?"

Jem nodded.

"And that's it?"

"Yep."

"Done. Miss Triumph here we come."

We both raised our hands and smacked them together.

chapter twenty-two

"Now," said the psychologist man. "We're going to play a game."

I said nothing. Instead, I stared back into his glasses. Found his eyes. In my head I squeezed them tight into nothing.

He got out some big cards.

"I'd like you to tell me what they are?"

I didn't reply.

Mom said I had to come back. Just for a few more times. I was counting. So far there'd been three more times. How many was a few more times? Not past six I decided.

A card was held up.

"A cow."

Another card.

"Another cow."

The doctor sucked in a breath. I held on to the chair. He was trying to suck me into him. I wouldn't let him.

"This one."

"A rooster."

This was so dumb. The drawings weren't really drawings. They were just thick black lines. They could be anything. I just said the first thing that came into my mind.

"A pear tree."

"Why pears?"

"We've got one at home. It's in the backyard. Some of it hangs over the fence. Those hanging things look like pears." Whoever did those pictures wasn't a very good drawer.

"Last one."

"Two people kissing."

"Good." The cards were put down. He wrote something on his pad.

Mom and Dad don't kiss much. Only sometimes. I've seen Jem watching them carefully, as if trying to learn how to do it himself. What's he want to kiss anyone like that for? Yuck.

As soon as I crawl out of the worm tunnel, it vanishes. Like it was never there.

I'm lying on a hillside. In long, luscious, beautifully scented grass. I scoop up the green perfume in my hands and breathe it in deep. The smell is young and happy. Above me lies the sky.

I ROLL OVER ONTO MY STOMACH.

THERE'S A STREAM NOT FAR AWAY. I SIT UP, EXCITED.

If it's the same stream in Hoodman's picture on the wall, it will lead me to Jem.

"So, here you are."

I jump. I know without looking who it is.

Morven. Poaching me like a cold shadow, his eggy eyes hanging loose in his face. A trail of gold glints in his top teeth.

Dread fills me. How'd he get here? I take a step back.

"It's hopeless," he says with a sick smile, "to try and escape. Surely, you realize that by now. Escape can only happen after you've admitted what you're hiding."

I kick out at him. Thrust my foot hard. "I'm not hiding anything. I haven't done anything wrong. I don't know what you're talking about." But even as the words are there, I feel something stirring within me. Almost as if I know exactly what is he talking about.

He moves aside.

I dig my fingers into my pocket, find my eraser. I got rid of him once, I can do it again.

"It's no good," he says.

"What isn't?"

"You rubbing me out." He sighs. "Such a silly waste of time."

"Yeah? Well . . . we'll see about that." I start to rub out his face.

His big, flat hands make a grab at the eraser. It goes spinning to the ground.

I drop down, scrabble around in the long grass.

Where is it? I mustn't let him get it.

Then he's beside me. Morven, scratching around. Morven, with his half-erased face.

My fingers land on something small and soft. It's the eraser. I snatch it up. Quick as I can, I rub over his searching fingers.

Now he's handless with one white and undercooked eye.

I laugh out loud as I get rid of him completely.

Least that'll give me some more time.

"Jem," I yell. "I've got your cap. See." I wave it in the air.

There is nothing. No response.

He's near. I know it. Him and Hoodman. What's their game? It's driving me totally over the edge.

I want to stop. To give up. But it's too late for that. I'm not leaving the comic until I've found Jem.

NEXT I SKETCH a SMALL ROWBOAT.

When it's done, I push it into the fast moving river and jump in.

I'm rocked and bounced around. But I cling on.

"I'm coming, Jem."

Farther and farther I'm carried down the inky stream. The happy, blue sky turns to clouds.

Soon it's pouring.

"Come inside, Zara," called out Mom. "You're getting wet."

I was doing a rain dance. Our teacher told us all about rain dances and how when there were terrible droughts the people of those countries would do a dance especially to get it to rain. So that was what I was doing. It felt lovely. The rain wasn't cold. I tipped my head back. The drops landed plunk, plunk on my face. I twirled round and round with my arms outstretched, drinking in the dropping rain. My hands caught the rain. It slipped through my fingers. The grass was dancing with the rain. All around me it felt like I was caught in a rain web.

"Zara," called out Mom again. "For goodness sake. Will you come inside before you catch your death."

I didn't want to catch my death so I did what Mom said. Then I went into my bedroom and did a drawing of me dancing in the rain. It was a nice picture, but after I escaped from the man I ripped it up. It reminded me too much of the day when I went down the street with Melissa Summer.

Someone is steadying me. I feel a grip on my arm. I wiggle.

"Let me go, Morven. Let me go," I yell.

I yank my arm. But I'm not fast enough.

"It's all right, sweetheart. It's Grandma Sophie."

It can't be. You can't be her. Grandma Sophie's dead. She died when I was eleven. Her heart stopped one morning on her way to the bathroom.

"You got a bad bump on the head when you fell off the trampoline." Her arms pulled me close. Encircled me. "But you're fine now. I've got you."

I must have slipped inside a memory.

Or am I still in the comic?

I'm confused.

Warmth floods. Gentle tears fill my eyes, swell up.

Mustn't cry.

I long to lean my head against my gran's chest and be rocked.

Instead, I put my hands over my ears. Stomp my foot.

"It's you, Morven. I know it is."

My gran died.

The funeral for her was awful. Mom kept

sobbing. You could hear her gulping sobs all over the church. I tried not to hear her. In my mind I stayed perfectly still, sketching you in my head standing there beside the big arrangement of flowers. All smiley, like always.

"How's my favorite girl today?" Gran would ask when we came for a visit.

"Better now," I'd reply.

Grandma Sophie smelled of freshly baked scones, gingerbread, or pancakes, and happiness. I could smell her happiness, as long as I stayed safe in her arms.

See, I remember all that. So it isn't her.

Yet somewhere inside me I want to be wrong.

But I truly know that my gran is nothing more than flat pictures in one of our photograph albums.

Pictures don't have all those lovely happiness smells.

Because she took those with her when she went.

chapter twenty-three

The river curves.

Water sprays. Pings the air with ink beads.

I'm clinging to the edge of the boat, desperately wishing I'd thought to add some oars and a life jacket.

Spears of sun pierce the clouds. The downpour is done.

The river is getting narrower. Shreds of mist drift between the trees on either side of the water. Rocks rise from the surging current.

I'm in for it. I've nothing to steer the boat. The riverbanks are closing in. The boulders loom—large, threatening. I'm going to be ripped to shreds.

I fling myself out of the boat and into the water. Wait for the shock of cold to hit me. But the water is strangely warm.

"Listen," says Trace, *her voice quite clear in my head. "You know the pop idol thing that everyone has been going on and on about, well . . . guess what?"*

I bet I know.

"That total jerk Rodney has only put me in for it. Did it last thing so I wouldn't know. He's going to wear my fists."

Liar. You love the thought of being a rock star. Admit it.

"Yeah. It's okay for you. Hanging about like you're doing. But if I'm going to do this, I need you there. You listening to me?"

I hear Trace suck at the air.

"And guess what else? The rules say once you've chosen an artist you've got to stick with that person. No changing and no pulling out once you've entered. No excuses. Totally dumb. What happens if you end up in the hospital? You're going to do the idol stuff from your bed? Oh, ha-ha. Hardly."

Her chip bag is ripped open.

"As for trying to tell them it wasn't me who wrote my name on the list, well, that got dismissed quicker than Jack Wheeler."

Jack Wheeler. We used to call him the wheeler-dealer. He was always selling stuff. Not drugs, though. Cell phones, DVDs, and the like. Totally sad he got caught. Some of his deals weren't too bad. We haven't heard of him since. He's probably moved to another school and doing the same thing. A real entrepreneur in the making, as long as he stays out of jail.

"Hey, sleepyhead, I hope you're hearing all this."

Yeah. Yeah. Just get on with it.

"Dad told me he'd get me a guitar or whatever I wanted. Said his girl would have the best. How about that? Didn't call me a mistake for once. I'd say he's getting into this a bit heavy. I'm not bloody singing. Not for nobody. Not getting up there and making a fool of myself."

The chip crunching stops.

Whiffs of onion float on the silence.

"Mind you, when you think about it, I'd be heaps better than Marsha or Ryan and half the others. Yeah, I would, you know. You'd better believe it."

I open my mouth to tell her that I know she'd

be great. She mightn't think it but she would. I'm remembering the time she went crazy in class one day. When she stood on her desk and pretended to be Madonna. Madonna as a Goth punk rocker. But she's off again before I can get a word in.

"Ha. You know what. Might even change my mind on that. What a laugh if I did go for it. Imagine the faces. Marsha would probably wet herself."

More crunching.

"Anyway. And this is a biggie. Who would I be? And what the hell would I sing? Nah! It's too stupid. Not going to do it. Don't care what they say. Don't care what they threaten. So there."

I banged at the cupboard door. It didn't move. I did it again and again until my legs just couldn't anymore. I gave up.

Pretended I wasn't there.

Like the time I scribbled over my homework so it wasn't there and got told off by my teacher. But she didn't understand. The story I wrote was no good. It would have taken too long to rub it all out.

A scuttling sound. I lifted my head. Waited and listened. It was a soft scratching. Mice. Mom told me they were nothing to be afraid of. But I didn't like them. I didn't like their beady eyes, their long slippery tails, and their sharp claws. Silence. Had they gone? Or were the mice inside the cupboard with me? They wouldn't get me. They wouldn't. I curled up smaller and smaller until they were gone. Now they couldn't get me. I was not there. I was not anywhere.

Close by I heard breathing. It was jerky. Scared. It sounded all chopped up. Red with blood and seeds. The same as my lunch sandwiches, pale and stained with dead tomato.

When were Mom and Dad coming to get me? I was getting hungry. And Jem? But maybe Jem wouldn't come. He was mad at me for annoying him. He told me to go away and leave him alone.

So I went outside.

I danced and danced with the pink sparkly scarf until the woman came along. She wasn't a bit like her name. Summer is nice. She wasn't nice the way she hauled me behind the tall fence and dragged me into the lane beside the Mulhollands' place. I hadn't done anything wrong. I didn't know what she wanted. She told me she wanted the Mulhollands' house. Not the other place. She was lying.

Mom would have her for that.

She'd put mustard on her tongue. As she did with me. Like when Mom didn't believe me when I told her I took the money sitting on the dresser. She knew it was Jem. I covered for him. I had saved him from a fate worse than death. Didn't matter how much my tongue hurt, it was worth it.

Jem said he'd do the same for me one day.

STEAM SHIMMERS. STANDING ON THE EDGE OF THE RIVER IT STREAMS AND CURLS FROM MY CLOTHES.

It twists and forms a shape.

Dark Eagle.

The sound of wings—slow and powerful—fill the air.

"Wait," I cry. "Don't go. Don't leave me. Show me where I can find Jem. Please. I'm exhausted and don't know how much longer I can keep going. Please."

TALONS STRETCH AND PICK ME UP.

SWING ME HIGH INTO THE AIR.

Far below I see the river snaking between the hills. We are flying out of the picture that I saw in Hoodman's place.

All the time I hear Dark Eagle's voice.

"Not all is what it seems. Stop running. Let out the truth. Your truth. Find that door, open it, and let it find its own light and you will find Jem."

"Tell me."

"You know where he is."

"I don't. I've been trying and trying, but I can't find him."

The banging in my head begins, hammering away behind my brain.

"Please," I beg. "I can't do this anymore."

"Then don't."

His colors shine. They're so bright and dazzling I close my eyes. Shut them against the ache of him and the noise in my head.

"Here we go," yelled out Jem over the noise of the motorcycle's engine. "Hang on."

My arms gripped his middle.

We roared off the sand. Away from the wild waves with their angry lashing. Headed up and onto the road that ran along the top of the beach where tires had burned beneath the twisted, ancient fir trees. The noise drove deep into my head while sun splashed the canvas road.

"Aren't you glad I pestered you to come out?" I cried out with a laugh. "Go on, admit it."

But Jem didn't answer. He was too far into his own world.

"Don't go too fast," cautioned Mom when Jem first got the Triumph.

"Take it easy," said Dad.

Jem laughed and nodded and said to me, "Hop on, kiddo."

As I waved, I saw Mom and Dad getting smaller and smaller until they were two stick people in a drawing. The way I used to draw people when I was very little. But not anymore. For ages I've been drawing people pretty good. It's funny the way they come into my head and sit there until I draw them out. Sometimes my head feels crowded. Sometimes just one person comes in. Like the day when Melissa Summer arrived.

She just stood watching me from inside my head the same as she did that day outside our gate. With her big sunhat and sunglasses covering up her face. Her straw-colored hair, neat and tidy around her shoulders. Her lips colored in red, and wearing a cherry-red jacket. A spider sitting on her jacket. It sparkled, so I knew it wasn't real. But it looked kind of real. Black legs perched just like the spiders I'd found and taken to school to give to the teacher. After the fifth spider I was told not to bring anymore. I was told to draw them instead and bring the drawing.

One of my teachers had a big mark running

down the side of her neck. Josie, who sat next to me, said someone had tried to kill her once and that was where the knife had stabbed and slit her open. After that I couldn't stop looking at the mark. It was like that was all of her. She had no nose, eyes, or head or anything. There was just that mark.

I'm glad she never came into my head so I didn't have to draw her. There wouldn't have been anything to put on the paper except that ugly red and scrunched up line.

"Paul, isn't it? How nice you've come."

"Is she going to be okay?"

"Yes," says Aunt Chloe. "You know Zara. Always one to hang in there. Roses. What a gorgeous color."

"I know she likes them. She told me once."

Tell me he isn't great.

Aunt Chloe's never met Paul before. She'd only heard about him heaps of times from me before we split up. Not sure why he wasn't around when she was, but it doesn't matter now. Typical that she meets him after we're no longer together.

Lovely, darling, sweet Paul.

He's wearing that gorgeous aftershave lotion. The smell that used to drive me nuts. The one I would snuggle into. My head in the crook of his arm as we lay in between the sand dunes.

On our last time at the beach Paul rolled over and licked my neck.

"If you eat me up, there'll be nothing left," I warned him.

"Yum. I'm willing to risk it."

I laughed. Heard the soft murmur of the wild grasses. Yet there was no breeze. The world was still. The ocean quiet.

His hand moved under my T-shirt. Paused. His eyes searched my face.

I wanted him to touch my breast. I wanted to feel what it was like. I pretended I didn't know what he was doing while his fingers walked up to my bra. He paused again.

Inside, I was blushing. Feeling stupid. What if they weren't right? How could your own boobs not be right? How stupid was that?

"I'm not sure . . ."

He pulled his hand out, moved away from me, and fell back onto the sand.

"I didn't mean . . ."

What did I mean? I wanted him to; I didn't want him to.

I pulled myself closer to him, took his hand and pressed it against my breast.

"But nothing else," I told him my voice shaking, falling to pieces at the warmth of his touch. And at the shock of how good it felt.

chapter twenty-four

Dark Eagle has gone. Done his usual flap and disappeared.

That's okay.

I've decided to take a rest. That's what he said. Stop running. So that's what I'm doing.

I've drawn a piece of paper onto the ground and on it I've sketched our house. You can see my front bedroom window, and Jem's. It's just a bit along from mine. The house needs painting. It always has, for as long as I can remember. It's made of wood. Not brick.

Mom told me we should have got a brick house because that way it wouldn't need to be painted, but when she fell in love with this house she didn't care about it not being brick. Didn't care that it would need heaps of paint and attention. She just loved it right from the word go. Mom and Dad didn't take any vacations after they got married. They both saved and saved as much money as they could, and then just before Jem was born, they had enough money to put down on this house. It's not in the fancy part of town, but that's not Mom or Dad, or Jem and me.

Jem hated me drawing him. He'd tell me to get lost. There's a good one I did, though, of him reading a comic. Lying stretched on his bed with just the tip of his feet showing and his cap. In between is a comic. I made it so huge because that's where Jem always is. Inside one of them. He laughed at the drawing. It's up in my room, just to the side of the wardrobe. I even did an exact copy of the comic's cover that he was reading at the time. The one where Hoodman's holding a guy by the scruff of his neck. You can't see Hoodman's face, of course. Most of the time he's got his back to the artist. Anyway, I borrowed the comic after Jem had finished with it, with a pledge not to let anything happen to it. If Jem had his way, I'd have had to sign in blood for it. I was only taking it into my bedroom and back again. Truly, you have to know how totally berserk Jem is about his collection.

I glance up from the rough sketch of our house and look around. Dark Eagle has left me on an abandoned piece of flat land. I fold up the picture into a small square. Put our wooden house that needs painting into my pocket.

From the other pocket I pull out Jem's cap and place it on my head. I might as well wear it. Besides, you never know. When Jem sees it, he'll recognize It. He'll want it. He's never without his cap. It'll make him come to me.

Then I laugh out loud. Really laugh. I've had a brilliant idea.

No—I'm not going to draw a car. Though I suppose I could. Roar off into the shadowy distance.

I'm going to draw Jem.

I'm sure that's what Dark Eagle meant when he said "You know where he is." He's at the tip of my pencil.

Yet, I argue, that's got to be too easy.

Hasn't it?

chapter twenty-five

"Listen to this, Zara. That is if you can hear me."

It's Dad.

Of course I can hear you. Why wouldn't I be able to?

"How're you doing?"

Fine. Dad seems awkward, embarrassed. Anyone would think he was talking to thin air. As if I'm not there.

"Mom's told me to finish the garage, or else. This time she means it."

I really can't tell you how many times I've heard that before.

"Jimmy's going to help."

He can't be talking about Jimmy Mulholland. The eighteen-year-old, permanently out of work, Jimmy Mulholland. He'll ruin the bit of the garage that's already standing. Everyone knows how useless he is.

Hey! I shouldn't have said that. I shouldn't be so unkind. It's not fair to Jimmy. We all know he can't help it. Not after he fell out of a tree when he was four years old and bits crunched around inside his head.

"He offered, so I couldn't really turn him down." Dad gives a desperate sigh. "I know what you're thinking. But I have to give him a chance. He at least deserves that."

Last person who gave Jimmy a chance was Mrs. Botting, the green widow. We call her that because since her husband died she's been into environmental stuff. Jimmy offered to build her a compost box. He had only started when he nailed himself in the leg and had to be rushed to the hospital. Dad went over and finished the job for her.

Jimmy's hands seem to have their own mind, like they don't really belong to him. It seems his brain tells them something different than what they're really supposed to do. He's a nice, kind person, but totally hopeless when it comes to anything practical.

Except for baking scones, if he takes it real slow.

And telling jokes.

JEM STANDS IN FRONT OF ME.

He's not quite right, but it looks like him, except for his hair. That's always sticking up when he's not wearing his cap. His eyes should be darker. If I had color, they'd be blue. A dark blue with a hint of gray. The same as moving water in different lights.

"Talk to me," I say.

His mouth doesn't move.

I frown.

How come when I draw a boat I can get into it and sail off down the river? Yet when I want Jem to be real, he isn't.

He's got no heart, breathes a voice in my head.

Okay. So how do I draw in his heart?

You can draw it, but it won't mean anything.

You just said he's got no heart.

He has to live to have a heart. He has to have a heart
to live.

The rabble in my head is driving me stupid.

"Stop it," I yell, covering my ears. "He is living. I just drew
him. Make him talk to me."

A stirring of wind gathers around my ankles.

My throat tightens. I feel a surge of anger. I want to hurt
something, someone.

I kick out at Jem.

"Where are you?"

"Happy sixteenth birthday, sweetheart."

Mom leans over and kisses my cheek.

Is it really my birthday? I thought it was still
days away.

"I hope you like it," she says as she slips something
over my fingers and onto my wrist. "Trace helped me
choose. She said you'd been hanging out for it, or words
something like that. It's the bracelet you saw in
Markham's Jewelry shop. Do you remember it? She
said you were crazy for it."

Do I remember it?

Trace and I had been both drooling over the
gorgeous bling. Me in particular over the cut-crystal

bracelet. The prices in Markham's were enough to hurt your eyes and leave a lasting impression on your wallet. Mom and Dad must have won the lotto to have spent so much on me.

"When you're home again we'll have a big party. Balloons and streamers and champagne, and . . ."

"Hey," says Dad, *"come here."*

"I'm sorry. I promised I wouldn't cry, but I can't help it. She should be out celebrating with her friends. Not lying here . . . not . . ."

"I know," says Dad. *"I know."*

He tied the blindfold tight.

I thought it was a game, like that hide-and-seek game we played on my fifth birthday. It was scary hiding for ages inside my wardrobe. Ducked down behind my clothes. Crouched in a small ball on top of my shoes. I stayed there for a long time. I listened and listened for one of my friends to come and find me and shout out, "Found you." But they didn't. No one came so I pushed open the wardrobe door. The light pinged my eyes and the house had gone all quiet. I crept out of my bedroom in case it was a trick to get me. But there was no one there. Everyone had gone.

I tiptoed down the stairs as quiet as I could.

Then.

BOO!

I jumped into the air.

My friends giggled and laughed at me shaking like a jellyfish.

My skin turned all wrinkly from the fright. Tears jumped about inside my head. Big girls didn't cry on their birthday. Big girls who are starting school soon are brave and excited about everything. Even getting boo shouted at them.

But the cupboard wasn't a game of hide-and-seek. My eyes itched as the material dug into them.

Whispers hid behind me. Sneaked out when I wasn't listening. Crawled over my face and hair. Sneaked up my nose. Scuttled along my arms and legs. Go away, I whimpered. Leave me alone.

The whispers were there all the time.

The same as the blue door.

And the small round hole he peeped through.

I wanted to stick a sharp thing in it and spear his eyeball. Then I'd pull it out and watch the blood drip.

"It's very sad. Tragically sad."

What's sad? And what's Ms. Winter doing here? Come to test out my math?

"How's Trace coping?" asks Mom.

Who's she talking to? Me or Ms. Winter? My head's like a junkyard, where piles of stuff seem to be stuck, rotting away, blocking my thinking, and making it one big muddied mess.

"She's been quiet actually," says Ms. Winter. "Not her usual self. That is when she turns up."

"She's been coming in here every day."

"Yes. I thought as much."

A loud crash erupts nearby. Interrupts the voices for a moment.

"And how are you coping? It must be quite dreadful."

"Oh . . . yes . . . well, you know . . . when you have no choice . . ."

Somewhere I'm lying backward on the swing in our backyard listening to them talking. Am I still in the comic? I can't be sure, but I can hear voices. I'm concentrating on swinging back and forth, imagining that I have long hair and it is sweeping across the ground. The swing has always been my dreaming place. I like pretending that I'm a rich and famous artist. One who makes heaps of money from my art.

"You hear that, Toss. We're going to be famous."

Upside-down Toss barks.

"You and me and Jem are all going to be rich and famous."

"What did you have to eat?"

"Not worms and insects," I told the psychologist man. I folded my arms and smiled at him. Before Mom dropped me off, she told me to behave myself. I told her I always did. She shook her head and gave me a sad look.

It wasn't my fault that the man kept on asking stupid questions. I didn't want to be nice and good and well behaved. I didn't want to be here. So there.

"And to drink?"

I could tell he was cross. "Water sometimes."

"I'm not asking anything difficult, Zara. Just what you had to eat and drink. It's not a trick."

His voice felt like a finger poking at me. Jabbing holes in the air between us.

I shrugged. Swung my legs. Back and forth. Back and forth.

"I see." Dr. Beardsley leaned over and pulled open a drawer. He took out a handful of pens, all colors. "Then how about you draw what you ate."

He knew he had me.

"That's boring."

"Then draw what you want."

I felt his grumpiness. It was like he had stuck his tongue out at me.

I started with the big hat and then the sunglasses. Then came the spider, mustn't forget that. Lipstick. Heaps on her lips. The Melissa lady's puffy white hands, and the wobbly high heels. She was wearing a dark-colored coat. A blue or black. I couldn't quite remember, so I made it dark blue. I drew some spits of rain as well as some sunshine, because that's what the day had been like. Then I drew me in the yard with my sparkly scarf. I made the scarf float up in the air. It looked all fluttering and pretty. You could see the sparkly bits if you looked really carefully.

I bet the psychologist man won't see them. He didn't seem to care about things like that.

"Hey, girl. You still lying there? It's your birthday if you didn't already know. So what are we doing to celebrate? What? Nothing! Talk about a party pooper. I'll remember that next time you're wanting me to do the town over."

What's Trace talking about? We've never done the town over. She's threatened it enough times, but we've never actually done it.

"Anyway, anyone would think you're a celebrity or something. All these flowers and cards." Trace goes quiet. Then she starts up again. "You want a grape? Later maybe. I'll have some for you. Cheers!" Another small silence.

I can't be bothered answering. I'm too tired. All this looking for Jem seems to have worn me out. Maybe if I leave the search, he'll come home on his own. Maybe that's what Dark Eagle meant.

"Big day tomorrow," says Trace. "First round of the elimination for the pop-idol thingy. They've got to get it down to ten. Then five and then two. Hey! You following me?"

The thudding in my head bangs against the edge of my skull. I know I should make an effort to be there for Trace, but honestly I haven't got the energy right now. Just can't be bothered. Give us a few more days and I'll be there for you. I'll bring Jem with me and we'll hoot and scream and vote for you. Trace the Face. How about that? Good enough for you? Anyway what are you singing? Something slow and dreamy? Or something wild and punk? Bet it's the last one, right?

The thudding softens. Muslin thoughts move through my head.

I know Trace said she hates the idea of going in the competition, but underneath it you have to know she really yearns for the limelight. To be noticed. Otherwise why would she dress up her face in all that Goth makeup? And the black clothes. I've seen her real face; she's quite a looker. She told me she hates what she looks like. She says the mistake is right there in her face.

"Suppose you're wondering what I'm singing and who I'm going to be?"

She doesn't wait for a reply.

"'Heart of Glass.' Blondie. Our theme tune. Or have you forgotten?"

I haven't forgotten. The two of us bouncing around my bedroom screaming our lungs out until Jem flung open the door. Asked if anyone could join in or was it only those with talent. Of course he was being sarcastic. He stood there looking great and laughing.

Then something slips into my mind. Something I hadn't noticed at the time. Only now I do. I remember the look you gave Jem. You did, Trace. You know you did. I hadn't seen it then, but now

I see it as clear as anything. You fancy him. It was there all the time. Trust me not to notice.

"So . . . what do you reckon? Me as Blondie? A punk and Goth rock star! How about that?"

You'll be great. I wonder how long she's had this thing for Jem. Why hadn't I seen it before? Too close to my own nose I suppose.

"Yeah. It's going to be something to remember." Her laugh swings by me. "Trust me."

I can just see her and the judges. They have no idea what they're in for. Trace is going to be a sensation. If she gets no further in the pop idol competition, she'll give them something to remember.

Footsteps sound in my head.

"Hi."

"Oh, hi. I'm just going."

"It's Trace, isn't it? I'm Alex. You might have heard about me from Zara."

Yeah. She knows who you are. When I told Trace about Alex breaking up with Jem she made a fist and smacked at the air, calling her all sorts of names.

Now it makes sense. She hated to see Jem hurt in that way. Hated to see the ragged rawness Alex left. Never mind that it opened a chance for her. Except Jem's not into Goth, punk, or malls, or any of the stuff Trace is mad about.

"*They're nice,*" *says Trace.* "*Not that I'm all that big on flowers.*"

"*For her birthday.*"

"*Yeah. Right.*"

The conversation is like a scab I can't get rid of. I pick at it. My nail scratches in and out of it. Then I leave it alone. Instead, I let myself go until I'm spinning down and down.

I hear an ambulance. It sounds close. I'm circling into a light brighter than any other light I've ever seen. It holds me, pulls me gently into it. It's warm and comforting. I could stay in it forever.

"We're losing her."

Thump. Thump.

Don't. You're hurting me. I like where I am. Just leave me alone, can't you? I've got to find Jem. I know he's missing me. He needs to know I'm okay. I need to know he's okay.

Thump. Thump.

The siren screams inside my skull.

The wolf huffed and puffed, and puffed and huffed. Air rushes down my throat.

I weep inside my head. Why didn't they leave me where I was?

chapter twenty-six

I'm hanging over a shoulder like a carcass of meat. A dead animal with my head knocking against his back.

It's a big shoulder. Broad and strong.

It's Morven. It has to be.

I don't understand how I got here. Last time I looked, I was with Jem, the drawn version of Jem. I was wearing his cap. Now both Jem and his cap have vanished.

I must have fallen asleep.

It's like I have entered a prehistoric land. Grainy far-off hills, a leaking gray sky, leeched sand dunes. There's not a drop of color. I know I didn't draw it. I couldn't forget a place like this. It feels like a no-man's land. That stretch in between what is real and what isn't.

A place like this wouldn't be in any of the comics.

All Hoodman's adventures are in the city and they mostly happen after dark. The pictures are full of shadows and stark beams of light.

"I could rub you out," I say, my voice swinging from side to side with his stride.

No reply.

Then I will.

I reach into my pocket.

My heart stills.

The eraser isn't there. I must have dropped it, or left it lying back with the drawing of Jem, or lost it on the way.

I need it. I can't go on without it.

"Time's beginning to run out," breathes Morven. "You haven't long now."

I haven't a clue what he means.

Something gives my fingers a vicious nip.

"Ouch! You . . . you . . . leave me alone."

Morven laughs.

Beneath me his shoulder shrinks.
It wiggles and squiggles.

HE'S CHANGING INTO a SCORPION. I KNOW IT. I CAN FEEL IT.

I'M CLINGING ON TO THE HARD CRUST OF SHELL BEHIND ITS HEAD.

One flick of the tail and that's me done for.

Now we are skittering along.

It's like Morven was never here. There is only me and the scorpion. I want to leap off, but if I do, it will only make me an easier prey.

I really, really need my eraser and I curse myself for being so careless. Now I've got nothing to help me escape.

High above comes the sound of wings. I gaze up into the colorless sky. There is no Dark Eagle. Yet I know he's nearby. I feel his unseen presence watching, just as he does for Hoodman.

AS IF OBEYING SILENT INSTRUCTIONS, I PULL OUT MY PENCIL AND WITH a BRUTAL SWIFTNESS, I PLUNGE THE SHARP POINT INTO THE NECK OF THE SCORPION.

ITS TAIL STINGS THE AIR.

I flick myself out of the way, taking my pencil before I land on my feet in the sand. Feel its scorching heat sliding through my toes. A little ahead, the scorpion shrivels and disappears into the ground.

I stare at my feet. My shoes are missing. Where did they go? When did I lose them? Bits of me are falling off. Is that what Morven meant when he said that time was running out? The longer I look for Jem, the less there is of me. Then I need to hurry before there's nothing left.

This wasteland of nothing. Morven's bit of arid land. Home to the scorpion and other deadly creatures.

I do a drawing in the sand. The river with the mountains in the distance, trees, the boat, and Jem.

I cross my fingers, count one, two, three, and leap into the sand picture.

There's a large swooshing sound. I clamp my hands over my ears as I'm sucked down into the grains. They fill my mouth, cover my eyes, and travel up my nose. I can't cough or suck in air. I'll choke. I can't hold my breath much longer. Is this what it's like to drown?

I gulp and swallow water.

The sand is gone. I'm in the river clutching onto the edge of the bank next to where I landed the boat. I pull myself out and lie there.

Someone takes my hand. The touch is cool.

I look up. Kneeling beside me is Jem.

chapter twenty-seven

My head is full of music. I'm not sure where it's coming from. Perhaps it's what Brian brought in for me to listen to. Yes, that must be it.

The notes float above me. I want to reach out and pull them down and keep them safe.

As Mom and Dad wanted to do with me.

It was Mom who was too scared all the time.

Making it like being back in the cupboard.

Where a pillow and blanket were shoved in with me. They smelled old. Like they hadn't been used for a long time. Hidden away until they'd grown spots of mold. I didn't use them at first, but then I did. My head and body were sore from lying on the wood. The blanket was thin, worn out from hiding or covering someone. I didn't like it near my face. It made me want to be sick.

I don't know why the man wanted me. He didn't hurt me. He gave me food. I didn't eat it at first, because I thought Mom and Dad would come

and get me. They would find me. Then I did eat
because I was hungry and because they didn't come.
Sometimes it was noodles in a mug; sometimes
it was a bit of toast with jam and a drink of hot
chocolate.

First came the asking, the whispering, making
sure my eyes were covered, then the scraping of the
blue door, the quiet footsteps, finally the soft sound
of the cupboard lock being undone and food being
pushed inside, then the door closed and locked.

My legs and arms got cramps really bad a lot of
the time.

In the end I didn't care much about anything.

It was like Mom and Dad hadn't ever been
around. They were just some people I had met
once. I tried to keep them inside my head, but they
kept floating away. Farther and farther. Smaller
and smaller until the bright picture of them both
outside laughing, or at the kitchen table talking,
was nothing, just a smudge on the inside of my
head. I even had trouble trying to remember what
Jem looked like. Mostly, I could just see his comics,
lying in a pile on the floor beside his bed. Then
one by one they disappeared, like someone had
taken them away and put them somewhere else so I

wouldn't see them. And Toss. Perhaps I made him up. Perhaps I made them all up. Perhaps all the time this was where I was born, inside this cupboard.

Except one day the man must have been in a hurry because when I stretched my leg against the door, to stop the cramps from coming, it moved.

Sparks flew about in my head.

I wanted to get out of the cupboard, but I was frightened. It might be a trick to get me.

I gritted my teeth. Felt the ache in my stomach start up. Heard the pounding inside my head.

What if I was being given a special chance to escape? What if Mom and Dad and Jem and Toss were real? And the only thing that wasn't real was me being kept in this place? The thought hammered around my head.

I wiggled and wiggled at the door like I did when one of my teeth got loose, until all of a sudden it popped open. I sat there shaking. Too frightened a hand would come and slam the door closed again. I put one leg out of the cupboard. Then the other. Shuffled out on my bottom. Halfway, I remembered about the pink sparkly scarf. I couldn't leave that. I scrabbled around and found it and held on to it tight, but left the blindfold.

The room was in darkness. My legs wobbled as I crept over to the blue door. I heard footsteps. They were coming. Getting nearer and nearer the room. My heart banged against my chest. Spots floated around my brain. Blues and pinks and yellows.

I couldn't let him find me. I sucked in a breath. Crouched down behind the blue door and waited. But the steps didn't come to the room. They went somewhere else. I reached up and turned the doorknob. I peered out. The man wasn't there. I took off. Out the blue door, out another door at the far end of the passage, and then out into the darkness.

"Hey! Listen to this, girl. Blondie and me, we got into the final fifteen for the pop idol. Yeah. How about that? Course there was some shit stuff, but there were some others who weren't half-bad. Me included, of course." Trace laughs. "Pity you had to miss it."

Yeah. Yeah. But I'm a bit busy right now. I've told you Jem and I will be there for the big finale. So you'd better be in it. You hear me?

"You know that Jenny Crowther, well, everyone just loves her. She's okay. But when it comes to the school voting at the end, she'll get in because of that. Talk about stink. And Tom Richards . . . wow . . . he's so amazing.

Reckon he could pull it off. He's into Justin Timberlake big-time. You should have heard him sing. You wouldn't think he had anything in his head or in his pants, but boy has he one cool voice."

Trace sounds interested. That is a big surprise. I think of Jem and how I never realized she was a bit more than interested in him. Now Tom. She needs to get rid of the Goth image and be herself. No hiding behind the painted pale face and all the dark stuff. That way the guys might take to her.

"Anyway, like it or not, I'm gonna read you the article that Lisle Cameron wrote about the first round of the competition to weed out the no-hopers. Lisle's a bit of a wannabe rock dude, but, hey, we can't all have such talent."

At that, I imagine Trace grinning.

"Listen to what Lisle calls herself: Your Very Own Pop Reporter. Ha!"

Get on with it, Trace.

Trace clears her throat. "Yesterday afternoon the gymnasium rocked to the sounds of the pop idol. This popular competition drew over sixty hopefuls. Song entries were as varied as Madonna, Justin Timberlake, and Elvis Presley."

Trace pauses, then says, "Heaps of acts were so totally lame. That's me saying that, not Lisle."

Yeah. Yeah.

"With the first elimination, entries were culled to fifteen instead of ten. When asked why, Mr. Cross volunteered to say, 'In the final count several individuals gained the same number of points, consequently making the number swell.'"

I hear the piece of paper Trace is reading from rustle.

"Now listen to this. It'll make you laugh."

I'm listening.

"There was only one minor disturbance when Eddie Bannister threw his guitar at Ms. Winter because of her insulting comments about his singing."

I yawn inside my head. How much longer, Trace?

"The only damage suffered during this unruly incident was to the guitar. Rumor has it that Eddie Bannister is banned from playing cricket until the end of the year. Only the one thing he's good at."

Eddie Bannister is a bit weird. Last year he shaved his hair and got a tattoo of a lawnmower on the top of his skull. Now that his hair has grown back, you can't see the mower.

"Poor bugger. It's Winter that should be punished. Anyway, just in case you hadn't worked it out, the band doing all the backing is none other than the school's very own Riverstone Blue Hearts."

Trace sighs.

"So you'd better believe it when I tell you there's some mighty competition. But you know what? I never thought I'd be hanging out for the next round. But I am. Silly, eh? Especially when I'll probably get voted out."

Don't say that. Don't even go down that road. You can pull it off; I know you can. My eyes fill with moisture. I feel sad. I don't know why; it's like I know something, but can't figure out what it is and it's making me sad.

"Hey! Changing the subject. Saw your dad today. Dropped by to say hi and you'll never guess what. Him and that Jimmy Mulholland are working on the garage. Yeah. Hard to believe, eh? That garage has been sitting unfinished for forever. In my book it's kind of been a memorial to all those half-built garages. Now all of a sudden it's being finished. Wow!"

I know. Tell me about it. Still, it'll be great for Jem to have somewhere finally to keep his precious bike. Ever since buying it, he's been worried about someone stealing it. You have to laugh. What? I told him, that old piece of metal? Not likely.

"And you've got to hand it to those motorheads, who your dad's helped at the garage, for giving the gear. They are really hanging in there for him and your mom."

I wonder how Mom and Dad are paying for the garage. Sudden-like, after all this time. Not sure I understand why they're doing it right now though. But Trace is right. Dad's always helping guys with their car problems with a smile as if it's the best job in the world.

"So how are you doing? Here's me going on and on about my stuff and you not saying a word. You always were too polite for your own good."

Was I? Am I?

"Oh. Hey. Hi, Paul."

"Hi, Trace. Anything different?"

"Same old, same old. Here, you can have the seat; I'm just going."

"Wanted to say you were pretty amazing as Blondie."

"Listen! If you're after my body, you haven't a chance."

Paul laughs.

chapter twenty-eight

The touch of Jem's hand fades. I blink against the glare of light. Where's he gone?

"Jem," I cry out.

"Her pulse is low."
"Okay. Lift on the count of three."

Jem's gone.

But he was just here.

I swear it.

"One, two, three."

"Jem, where are you?"

Somewhere far off there's a high-pitched screaming noise. Make it go away. I want Jem. Where is he? I want to be back on the motorcycle, sand surfing, then up onto the road where the pine trees lean dark and the sun spikes the road.

Rocking, rocking.

Someone takes hold of my hand.

Leave me alone.

"It's okay. You're okay now."

You're not getting away with it, Jem. You and your stupid teasing games. Not this time. I'm too old for them. You hear me?

I stand up.

Walk away from the spot.

What is it I'm trying to remember?

It's important.

I know that much.

Of course.

The eraser.

I lost it.

Then I glimpse it lying on the sand. I bend to pick it up but it's too heavy to move. It's like it's been anchored, or my fingers aren't working.

"No," said the psychologist man. "I don't have an eraser. Besides you don't need one."

I glared at him. I did so need one. And I knew he had one. I'd seen it in his drawer. I pulled my mouth tight and folded my arms. Too bad. Now I wasn't ever going to finish the drawing.

"You never saw anyone else besides the woman?"

I don't answer. Don't say anything about him. That's because I never ever saw the man. So I'm not lying. I only heard his whispers. He was like a whispering ghost. There was only one time he didn't whisper. That was the first time I tried to escape and he caught me and when he grabbed me from behind, he covered my eyes with his big horrible hands so I wouldn't see him. That time he yelled at me.

"You've been a very bad, bad girl," he shouted as he shoved me face first back in the cupboard where the blindfold was, and slammed the door closed.

That time the girl lay very still.

I was not her. Zara had gone. She had been broken into a million pieces. Like her grandma's china doll. When the wind took it and smashed it onto the ground.

"Don't lie," said Grandma. "We don't lie in this family."

The doll's hanging eyes stared up at me.

I didn't do it. I promise, I didn't.

The man's voice sucked at the stale air through the peephole. "You will never run away again. You hear me? Tell me you will never run away again."

"I will never run away again." The answer came from the girl hidden in the dark cupboard.

Crumpled, like she had fallen from high up on the windowsill. Crumpled, with her eyes hanging out of her head. Bits spread around the ground. Shell bits. All tramped down now. All gone.

All broke.

"I only saw the lady," I told the psychologist man. You have to tell the truth. And that's what I was doing. I wasn't lying. I never saw him. It was just the Melissa lady. I swung my legs. Banged the toes of my shoes against the desk.

"Not one other person?"

He gazed over at me. His hands under his chin like his head was made of concrete and it was too heavy for him to hold. I could have drawn him like that. The picture filled my mind. My fingers wanted to get busy with the felt pens, but I didn't unfold my arms.

"Tell me, Zara. What do you like?"

I shrugged.

"Besides drawing."

"Nothing."

"Nothing at all?"

"Not being here."

I see a piece of glass lying next to my left foot. I bend down and pick it up, being careful not to cut myself on its sharp edges. I'm about to toss it when something inside the glass moves. I peer closer. It's me. Dancing and singing on the front lawn. Happy as I fling up the sparkly pink scarf into the air. It sits above me. Floats. I move the glass and I'm gone. For a fraction in time I was there, as I was, all that time ago. Now that little girl has long gone, never again to be the same.

I slip the fragment into my pocket. It seems important I take it with me. Keep the image close.

Somewhere Mom cries. Weeps as if she can't stop. I feel her tears dripping onto my cheek. They are warm like the rain the day Melissa Summer came.

"Listen, sweetie, I don't want to alarm you but your dad's like a madman. It's this garage thing. He's going at it full tilt. Jimmy, who's helping, isn't much good, but at least he's there. Such generosity from those guys, giving all the materials. Guess after that, he's had to show he's willing."

Why's Dad so intent on getting the garage done? It's stood for years like it has. It got started when I was nine. I frown. Doesn't make sense. The only way it would ever get finished, Mom used to say, was if they were going to sell the house.

I jerk. Feel a shudder jolt down my back.

They wouldn't do that. They both like living there. No. There must be some other reason for getting the garage finished. Perhaps some important person is visiting the street. I chortle. Yeah! Right. Hardly down our street.

"I hear that Trace is doing well in the singing competition they're having at school. She's a case and a half that one. But a loyal friend, I'll give you that."

I can't imagine life without Trace. Though in the beginning she used to bug me something terrible. The way she dressed and acted. I told her once to be herself.

"What?" she exploded. "Be an accident." Then she went and lay down in the middle of the road. Okay, it wasn't a really busy road, but still.

"Don't be stupid," I told her, trying to walk away and leave her there, but knowing she'd be stupid enough to stay until a car came.

"You want to see what an accident looks like?" she shouted. "Then hang around."

"Please," I said, "get up."

At that she turned her face away from me.

I stood there not knowing what to do. Then I

realized there was only one answer.

I went and lay down beside her.

"You total shit," she hissed.

"Yeah. Thought you'd like it."

A car came toward us, tooting its horn.

"Screw you," Trace yelled, jumping up and dragging me with her.

Walking down the street a bit later she said, "Let's go kick some ass."

Which in her language meant "let's go to the mall and suss out who's hot and what's happening."

"Honestly, you'd think they'd serve a decent cup of coffee in this place. They've had plenty of time to get it right. But it's obviously beyond them. Same old plastic cup with watery liquid. Next time I'm bringing my own. See if I don't." Aunt Chloe sighs. "Where are you, Zara?"

Why does everyone keep on asking that? I'm here, I shout.

Here. Can't you see me or something?

"Oh yes, that nice boy you used to go with. Now what's his name . . ."

Paul.

". . . Paul. That's right. Well, I saw him the other day. What a really nice person."

You know what? After I've found Jem, I'm going to go to Paul and tell him how I feel about him. It's not going to be easy. He might just laugh at me and walk away. Too bad. It's something I've got to do. It was unfair what I did, the way I treated him, when he'd been nothing but decent to me. When I told Trace, she just nodded, but didn't say much. Of course, she was fiddling with her cell at the time. Sending text number seventy-four for the day. I've no idea who she sends all those messages to. She's told me it's none of my business.

Aunt Chloe kisses my cheek.

"Okay, sweetie, gotta go now. You be good. Okay. No getting up to something I wouldn't approve of. Love you."

Love you too.

Who's there?

I hear quiet breathing.

"Hi, Zara."

It's Paul.

Hi.

He doesn't say anything else. It makes me feel kind of weird. Why doesn't he speak? He seems to be down in the dumps. What's happened to make him like that? I don't want to feel his pain so I pull back to when we were happy.

Right from the start, Paul had a way of touching my hand that gave me the shivers. It was just a small touch. He would do it when he thought no one was looking. It was our secret.

Except Trace knew. She told me she'd spotted it. I told her not to get mad. She said she wasn't and, hey, good on me for finding someone I really liked. She said it didn't bother her, but I felt her misery even though she acted like it was okay.

There's my eraser. This time when I go to pick it up, there's no problem.

I set to work.

I rub out the river, the trees, and the sand to see what's underneath. Beneath it all. Nothing. It's just blank. I seem to have been here before. I rub away until I've made a hole big enough for me to crawl inside. This has to lead me back into the comic. I've probably found the outline that surrounds the pictures.

I crawl and crawl. At last, I see a small dot of white. I keep heading toward it.

Please let me be back in the comic. Even Hoodman's room. Anywhere. So I can get to Jem.

The white dot spreads and grows. I crawl into a lot of white. The strange light hurts my eyes. It's so dazzling I can't see where I am.

"Good. You've found your way back."

My heart dives. Morven. He's always waiting for me. Any escape seems to be futile.

"We need to talk. It is getting urgent now."

"No, we don't. The only person I'll talk to is Jem. You hear me. I'm not telling you anything. Or Mom or Dad. Only Jem, which is why I need to find him."

"Come along."

"No."

I try to go backward, reach back into where I was. But I'm not fast enough. A soft, paltry hand reaches out and takes mine. Closes around it carefully.

"Where are we going?"

"Back to where it all began."

"No," I scream. I tug and try to free myself. "I'm not going there. I've told you I don't want to."

"You need to."

"The only thing I need is Jem."

I spit in the direction of the voice and hope it lands in his eye. Then something strange happens. Morven's grip is no longer there. My hand is free. Morven and the brightness of the light starts to fade. Shadows cling to the sides. They

seem familiar, but I can't place them. It seems too hard to remember anything.

"She's becoming restless."

"Is that a good sign?"

"It could be."

I'm burning hot. My eyes see nothing but the blue door. It watches me. I'm burned into the blueness. The door waits all the time without taking a breath. My eyelash flickers, closes, shuts out the blue. It's better that way.

"Zara."

Mom's voice is gentle. It's like she's pulling back the curtains in my bedroom and letting in the early morning sun.

"Remember when you were a little girl and you couldn't skip using the rope? You got so mad because both your hands wouldn't work together."

What's Mom talking about that for now?

"And how you fought and fought and never gave up?"

How could I forget? Two days it took me to master the simple art of skipping. Totally tragic. But I didn't stop just because I couldn't do it.

"That's what you need to do now. Don't give up. Be like then. Please, Zara."

Mom's right. I need to keep going just like I did with learning how to skip until I find Jem.

"We miss you so very much."

I won't be much longer. Here, I tell her, pulling out the fragment of glass. Take care of this for me.

chapter twenty-nine

I've seen him. Hoodman. He was standing in the shadows watching me. I'm totally sure it was him. One hundred percent positive. I didn't see his face, no one ever has, but he was here with his robe swirling, the way it does in the comics. Just like that. But when I tried to see him better, he had gone.

Still.

I know I'm getting close to finding Jem.

It was a sure sign.

That means I'm back in the comic.

Now the light and shadows are moving, shifting, something is opening up all around me.

I hear traffic. It sounds like a city. Ten steps and I would be in the middle of a busy street. People are hurrying both ways. I nearly get knocked over in their rush to wherever they are going. I move backward toward one of the tall buildings.

"Please," says a woman as she hurries by, "this is for you."

Swallowed up in the moving colors of coats, scarves, and hats and traffic lights, car lights, and flickering Christmas lights strung in front of the shops.

It's not Christmas. No wait. It could be. But I don't remember a Hoodman comic having Christmas in it.

The piece of paper hurts my hand. I open my fingers. It's changed into a fragment of glass. It's dug itself deep into my flesh. I yank it out. It comes with hurting, a long slim fragment. I glance at it. Two words flash at me. *Go back.* I shake my head. Go back to where? "If I do," I say out loud, "will I find Jem?"

"He's waiting for you. He's been there all the time."

The words aren't mine. I'm not even sure if they're real. They feel silken as they slip through my thoughts. "Take me to him," I beg.

"That is for you to do alone," comes the reply. "Follow what was and it will lead you. Go back to the beginning . . . back to when it all changed . . ."

It sounds like Dark Eagle and one of his puzzling answers.

The noise of the traffic disappears. The crowd melts away. I'm standing on my own on an empty footpath. The Christmas lights have stopped blinking. Now they are nothing but dead lights. Dead lights. Where have I heard that before?

Go back to the dead lights.

It repeats in my head.

Go back to the dead lights.

I was back to running with the dead lights. The car had gone; now the whole place was still, silent. How could I find my way home if the lights were dead? Somewhere I heard my mother playing the piano. Her music had found me. It found the inside of my head and stayed there. Sad music, like her fingers were pulling me along. I ran. I didn't need any lights. I heard the match on the radio. I heard Jem as he flicked over the pages of his comic. They were in time with the tune, in time with the cricket announcer. My feet heard them; my feet followed them, faster and faster. Nobody was behind me. This time he wasn't coming. He still didn't know I had gone.

My eyes didn't see anything. My ears didn't hear. I wasn't there. I was running with the dead lights and the rain coming down, making me wet.

Not tripping once. Playing tag with Jem. When I never got caught. When I always dodged him.

I ran round a corner and the lights came alive. It was my street. Where I used to live. Where I used to play and walk and have fun with Toss.

The music in my head got louder. It didn't let me go. It had me, like the cupboard, except it wasn't the cupboard anymore; it was Mom and Dad and Jem.

The banging on our door made me tired. My arms seemed stuck. I sank down onto the mat.

Yellow filled me. The hall light filled my eyes and ears and slid all the way down to my toes.

"Oh my God. Zara!" Mom kneeled down and wrapped me in her arms. "Is it really you?" Her warm breath wept against my cheek. Pressed deep into my skin.

Then Dad was there.

And Jem. I saw him grinning like I'd just scratched my knee or something and was being a baby about it.

Dad bent down, lifted me up, and carried me inside. All the time shaking his head. All the time saying nothing.

All the time just carrying me.

chapter thirty

"*Hey, Sleeping Beauty, you want to hear something great?*"

Hey, yourself. I thought you'd forgotten me.

"*You are now in the presence of a superstar.*"

Oh, really? You think so?

"*Yeah. Well. Not quite a superstar yet. But not far away. Anyway, get a load of the latest from Lisle about the pop idol competition. I'm gonna read what she's written, just so you can appreciate what talent there is sitting next to you.*"

Get on with it.

"*Pop idol contest whittles down to five. Playing to a packed audience, the fifteen finalists gave it all they had. Two standouts were Justin Timberlake and Blondie.*"

I never doubted.

"*Ahem!*" says Trace, clearing her throat. "*How about that! Standout. Me . . . or should I say Blondie.*"

Yay! Brilliant. I knew you could do it.

"*No cheering or clapping please. Not until I've finished reading the whole report.*"

I wish I'd been there to see you.

"Here is a list of the final five idols. Blondie (Trace Carson), Justin Timberlake (Tom Richards), Katy Perry (Samantha Tonkin), Eminem (Antonio Matais), and last, but not least, Lily Allen (Jenny Crowther).

Expect five outstanding performances.

Expect five new songs.

Expect to be wowed as the five are reduced to two.

Don't forget to be at the gym next Tuesday after school.
Come and vote for your pop idol."

I hear Trace shifting about on the chair.

"So what do you reckon?"

Blondie's going to win.

"You think I can pull it off?"

No sweat.

I'm standing on the pavement wondering what happened to the city, when an arm grabs me. Pulls me roughly from behind.

"Let me go," I yell, struggling to get out of the unexpected hold.

Hateful Morven.

"You reckon?"

"I do."

I feel my shoulders crack under his grip.

Then he pushes me away. "This way."

We're back in the middle of a white nothingness. It must be a clean page that holds no words, no images. If there's nothing on the page, then I can make it into what I want.

Can't I?

I walk. Glance over my shoulder. Look for my footprints. There aren't any. How strange. Perhaps it's because I'm sinking lower and lower into the white with every step. Soon it'll be too late. There'll be nothing left of me, and I'll never find Jem. No one will ever really know what happened to me.

"This time you will tell us the truth." Morven appears and slides next to me.

Ah, so that's it. It's all about telling the truth, Is it? Well, screw you.

I'm disappearing fast. I won't give in. Doesn't matter what they do to me.

"What did you do to Jem?" he breathes.

"Nothing."

His hand grips my arm.

"Why do you want Jem so badly?" I spit at him.

"I don't. But you do."

My head is starting to ache. I've no idea what he means. Of course, I've been trying to find Jem. That's never been a secret. So why take me? What is it he wants?

"So tell me, what did you do to Jem?"

"I don't know what you're talking about," I yell. The hammering in my head gets louder.

Morven shakes me. "Say it." His voice ices inside my ear, like the chill of a wind.

"Say what?" All of this is making me exhausted.

"Say what you did to Jem."

"I didn't do anything. Not unless you count me pestering him to take me for a ride."

"Still you continue to resist."

And then, I see her, the other Zara, the scared little girl. The one I left behind, the one I entrusted to Jem when I told him everything.

But that can't have anything to do with all this. Can it?

I feel myself slipping further and further into the white shroud. I go easily. I don't fight. I sink happily into oblivion.

AS I DO SO, I FEEL THE BRUSH OF DARK EAGLE.

Feel the greatness of his wings somewhere above me. He knows where Jem is, I'm sure of it. I just don't understand why he won't take me to him.

"She has so much talent," my teacher told Mom. "But it needs to be developed."

I knew what Mom was thinking. The same teacher, Mr. Bennett, had told her this before.

I'm eleven and a half. One more year at primary school, then onto high school. What Mr. Bennett was trying to tell Mom was that I needed to go to a special school where art was the main focus. I wanted to. Art's all I cared about. But we didn't have the money for those types of schools. So I said nothing. I didn't beg or scream or be a crybaby about it. I knew there was no use; I understood that. Besides, I liked living at home. I didn't really want to go and live somewhere else. Not even for art. I liked staying with my family. I liked my bedroom. It had everything I needed.

"Yes," said Mom with a wide acknowledging smile. The smile that meant she was feeling guilty. Except she shouldn't. It wasn't her fault they didn't have stashes of cash. And it wasn't Dad's either.

"I could go to a night class," I said.

Mr. Bennett's face sagged. "With your flair and understanding of art you need more than that." He knew he had lost. "There are scholarships Zara could apply for. I'm sure . . ."

"We'll think about it," said Mom. Then moved the conversation away from me and my art. "I hear you're moving on to fresh pastures yourself."

"I am. It's time for a change."

You're not selling the house are you? Dad, tell me you're not. Tell me that's not the reason for the sudden finishing of the garage.

"It's nice outside today," says Dad. "But I suppose we'll pay for it tomorrow. Get snow or hail."

Not yet. It's still early autumn.

"Scarsdale lost again." His voice droops.

Scarsdale's our local cricket team. Dad used to coach them once. And not only that, he used to play. Until he did something to his back and then couldn't run half as fast as he used to. He got presented with a cup for his batting when he was a teenager. Long before he met Mom. When he had shoulder-length hair and it was tied back in a ponytail. It's hard to believe it now, the way his hair is thinning on top. I tell him it's all the hard thinking he does and that he needs to lighten up.

"Your Aunt Chloe keeps threatening to give up her business. Says it's getting rough out there in the business world. But what else would she do? She'd go crazy, that's

what. And drive us there as well. Better to stay with the advertising, never mind what the economic times are saying. She loves it, even if she does bitch about it all the time. Can't ever see her making a garden or knitting a sweater. Nope, she's better off where she is."

Dad's right. Aunt Chloe loves the corporate world with a passion. Although when you really think about it, it's not really corporate. You have to live in a big city for that, but she knows advertising and how to make it work.

"Mom's at a work protest meeting. It's to do with management wanting to cut wages. Nothing different there," *he adds with a sigh.*

I feel myself getting angry. Mom works really hard at the supermarket and is always doing extra and doesn't get a big wage. It stinks. Makes me mad. When I've asked why she doesn't get another job she tells me she likes what she does and the staff. What she really means is that she's not good enough for anywhere else, except she's not saying it, not admitting it to anyone, not even to herself. She's been at the supermarket since leaving school at sixteen. So it's like a second home; anywhere else would feel foreign to her. Mom doesn't realize she could do anything if she set her mind to it.

"Anyway, the garage is coming along."

Yeah. So I heard. Why's it important to get it finished?

"I have to say that Jimmy's proving okay." Dad chuckles. "At least he's good at fetching and carrying."

A small silence encircles the two of us. Drops down between the conversation and lingers.

I feel Dad take my hand. He says nothing, just holds my hand.

The same way he carried me in his arms after I arrived home when I'd gone missing.

chapter thirty-one

"Now," said the young policeman, "there's nothing to be afraid of." He showed Mom and me into a small room and then left. The room had gray walls and no windows. There was a table and some chairs. Mom and I sat down at the table.

I looked around the room and decided I didn't like it very much. I wouldn't ever want to draw it.

We sat there for a while.

"Just tell the truth," said Mom.

I swung my legs. Counted how many swings before someone came into the room. One hundred and two. That's how many there were.

The door opened. A tall man came and sat down in front of us at the desk. He had a face a bit like Grandpa before he died and went to live with the angels in heaven. Except Grandpa didn't have such large teeth and he didn't wear such big glasses.

He smiled at me. "My name is Senior Sergeant

Robertson and I just want to ask you a few questions. Is that okay?"

I nodded and smiled back.

"Zara, can you tell me what happened? If you can, start from the beginning."

"I was playing with my sparkly scarf. We were dancing. I was throwing it up into the air and dancing around under it. It was all sparkly and lovely. It didn't matter it was raining. The spits were only every now and then."

I paused and gulped a deep breath right in the middle of the hollow silence that was inside the room.

The man waited. His eyes looked at me as straight as anything. It was like he had no blinks in him at all.

I started up again. "Then this lady comes and asks me where the Mulhollands live. Everyone knows where they live. Their house is really old and it's on the corner. Then she asks me to show her and I said I would and she says that I should tell someone where I was going and I told her I didn't need to because it was just down the same street and we didn't need to turn any corners."

"Was the person tall or short?"

I had to think for a moment. "She had on some high heels. They made her walk a bit funny."

The man's mouth twitched. "What else can you remember?"

"She told me she was visiting and lived somewhere else. That's why she didn't know where the Mulhollands lived. I liked her spider brooch. It looked real, and first off I thought it was alive, but it wasn't."

Beside me, I felt Mom shudder in her chair. I noticed her fingers twisting together. I didn't mind talking to this man with the big teeth. He was nice.

"When we got near the Mulhollands' place, I showed her the house. That's when she pulled me into the lane beside it and then into some bushes."

"The empty lot next to the Mulhollands' house? Before the corner?"

"Sometimes I used to go and play there with Melanie, but Melanie got sick and moved away. After that I didn't play there anymore."

The policeman raised his eyebrows.

"Mom told me not to."

"It wasn't safe," explained Mom. "People throw all sorts of rubbish there. Cans, bottles, used needles . . ."

"Quite. I understand."

"Then after that I don't know what happened."

"What do you mean?" said the man, leaning forward a little. His arms pushing on the table like the bulldozer machine that was outside the school once.

"She put something over my nose, stuffed it hard so I couldn't breath. I didn't understand why she did that when I showed her what she wanted." I had to stop talking. It made me feel horrible remembering that. Remembering the way the smell went right up into my head.

"Okay . . ." The policeman sat back in his chair and made his fingers into a steeple shape. "And after that?"

"I woke up with the horrible smell still in my nose. When I tried to sit up, I banged my head on something hard so I didn't try again. I wanted to go to the toilet but I had to hold on. I could feel some sides and a door. At first, I thought I was in a box and that it was all a big joke, but then I knew it wasn't a joke so I lay down and curled up in a small ball with the sparkly scarf, all cold and shivery and wanting to go to the toilet."

"And you couldn't see anything. Anything at all?"

"It was too dark."

chapter thirty-two

It was always the same when Jem arrived home on his bike.

First would come the roar echoing down the street. Then he'd drive up to the half-finished garage, and stop. Then he would push the bike by hand up the shell path and park it behind the garage. He did that so no one could see it. That's how crazy he is about it. As if anyone would want to steal it.

It was the same with his comics. Actually, when I think about it, I feel mighty sorry for the person he marries or anyone he gets together with. She is going to have a lot of pain in her life.

I reckon if he sold them all as a collector's item, he'd get hundreds of dollars, maybe even thousands. They are all in perfect condition and he has every Hoodman since they were first published twelve years ago. One a week. You can't imagine how many there are and how many boxes are lumping around the place, all carefully labeled with the dates and serial numbers. Mom has said she'll be glad when he leaves home, so he can take all of them with him.

If he sold them, he would be able to go on some fabulous trip to India, or Japan or wherever he wanted. Jem said he didn't care about going to any of those places; he was fine where he was.

Once, one of his friends (now a very ex-friend) took two of the comics without asking, as a kind of joke, but when Jem found out he nearly strangled the guy. Dad had to go round and take Jem with him to apologize because the guy's family were shouting about going to the police.

All over two comics.

So you can understand how his collection could never be taken lightly.

I learned that real early. No messing about.

"You listening, Zara?"

Yeah. Yeah.

"I'm telling you I'm totally freaked out over this pop thing. Never thought anyone would vote for me. It's like everything's changed. Kids keep coming up to me and telling me they love me. Sooo amazing."

I smile. Who's talking about being a mistake now?

"Even my sick family are with me on this one. Can you imagine that? Dad's talking it up big-time. Recording and stuff like that. Oh, ha-ha, I told him. It's like my lot never really saw me until all of this. Didn't have the faintest I could squeak out a half decent tune."

I hear Trace give a happy sigh. It's like for the first time she has found something she likes doing. Besides being a Goth. Maybe now she'll give that up.

"I told you about Marsha and Ryan being out before the first round. You know the duo that went solo. A total mess, both of them. You have to feel sorry. Anyway"— Trace pauses—*"forgot what I was going to say. Oh yeah. You know that Marsha wants me to win. Right. Like a hole in the head. That bitch has only been going round telling everyone to vote for Tom or Jenny and to stay away from me. Stupid cow. What! She didn't think I'd find out."*

So the finals. What's your choice?

"We've got to perform a different song for the big finale. A new one. God! Not sure what to do yet. I need to get it together though. It's going to be here real soon. Don't want to get caught out and give it all away. After all,

excuse me, I've got fans to think about."

The two of us laugh. It's like we're holding hands and skipping down the street. Just as the two of us did once, being silly, acting as if we were madly in love. Such stupid, lovely fun.

"And guess what? The big finale is open to the public . . . well, parents and friends and relatives. That gym is going to be bouncing. The Daily Times *is hooked up to come and the local radio station. Just as long as Channel Eleven doesn't show up. There's no way I want to be on TV."*

I listen to Trace. Listen to her happiness. Bubbling and burbling like a brew. It's something I've never really heard before.

It's always been held back, hidden behind the Goth mask.

Please, I beg, let me go. Jem will have to find his own way home.

I'm just too tired.

I did try, Jem. Truly. Maybe after a rest I'll be okay. I let out a long breath. Feel it pulling me along. Soft and easy.

"I'm sorry. At this stage there isn't anything else we can do for her."

Don't cry, Mom. I'm okay. Just tired. I'll be fine after a sleep. You'll see.

"Hello. And how is she doing today?"

"About the same," says Mom.

"I could offer a prayer?"

"Well . . ." says Mom.

"But only if you're agreeable."

"Perhaps . . ."

Mom, what are you doing? We never go to church. Except to a funeral, or if someone's getting married. Don't be a hypocrite.

"Yes, that would be nice."

The world's gone mad.

"Dear Lord, hear our prayer . . ."

Now I see a blue door, see it shimmering through the glass in the distance. I take out my eraser. I need to get rid of it forever.

I lift my hand.

"Don't." A force holds back my hand. "You need it."

I hate it.

"You need it to find Jem."

I know it is Dark Eagle talking even though I can't see him.

The blue door has nothing to do with Jem. It was that other business.

"It has everything to do with him," says Dark Eagle. "You gave Jem your pain, and he's held on to it for you for a long time, but now you need it back. The little girl of seven needs it; it belongs to her, to you, not him. Too often we hide away what we don't want others to see, pretending it isn't there. But always it remains, growing quietly in the moist darkness of our fear."

I put my hands over my ears so I won't hear that creepy man again. Always telling me how I was his baby doll, his child. How he loved me. How he needed to keep me safe from harm. The old whispers grow. Sprout behind the blue door until they are crawling out through the peephole and into my mind.

Telling me how his mother hated him. Wouldn't let him play with dolls or little girls. I heard his dribbling words squeezing through the blindfold. Felt them land on me, stick themselves to me, suck themselves into my head. I tried to pull them out when he wasn't around, but they kept on staying there. Sharp bits like glass splinters.

"In the name of the Father . . ."

I go up to the blue door, touch it with my fingers. Then I make a fist and push. Black anger erupts in my throat. I kick and punch at the door until it swings open.

There's nothing there.

Just an empty space.

Yet I can hear him breathing.

"I hate you," I scream. "Hate what you did to me."

I feel him reaching out to touch my hair with his spongy hand. The familiar frightened thudding rises, rips at my eyes.

"Such a good girl for Mommy. Because that's what I am to you now. Your mommy."

I crouch in a hole. Put my head on my knees. Warmth swells inside my head until it's got nowhere to go. My eyes burst.

"It wasn't what I wanted," I yell. "Everything was what you wanted. It wasn't ever my fault like you kept telling me."

". . . the Son and the Holy Spirit."

"None of it was my fault."

As soon as the thought is there, I hear the rush of Dark Eagle's wings getting fainter and fainter, until they're not there at all.

"Amen."

I turn away from the open door, the vacant and hanging blue, and I hear Jem calling my name.

"Zara."

He sounds faint.

Why now? I wonder. After all my endless hunting. Why has Jem chosen now for me to find him? Is it because I faced the blue door? Opened the hidden bit inside me?

"Zara." This time my name sounds closer. "I'm here."

Where's here?

"Open your eyes."

I pull them awake.

Am I in a dream? Or is it really his voice. If it is, then he's not far away. I knew I'd find him. Didn't I tell everyone I'd find him?

I feel myself walking down the shell path. Jem's bike is parked behind the garage. My feet are going crunch, crunch, like they're eating cornflakes.

"Where are you, Jem?"

Here.

The shells change into fragments of glass. The pieces are filled with color. I stoop and pick one up. My drawings. The glass is filled with my pictures. Why are they here all in pieces? I kneel down and gather up every sliver. Pull the pink sparkly scarf out of my pocket and wrap it around all of it. I tie a knot in the top to stop any from escaping.

A HAND HELPS ME UP. I SEE THE HOOD AND KNOW IT'S HOODMAN.

I GLANCE BEHIND ME. JEM IS THERE. RIGHT THERE.

HE NODS.

I'VE BEEN LOOKING FOR YOU.

"Everyone's been so worried. But I knew you were okay. I knew I'd find you. You are okay, aren't you?"

He smiles.

I feel his warmth.

"I'm sorry for being a pest," I tell him. "For pushing you into taking me for a ride. Next time tell me to butt out."

Hey. It's okay. You're not to blame.

I'm puzzled. "I don't understand . . ."

Jem continues talking as if I haven't spoken.

It's the same as when you were taken. You weren't to blame. But you know that now, don't you?

The inside of my mouth is wobbly, like it wants to cry.

Tell Mom and Dad what happened, Zara. Tell them like you told me. It will help them. It will help you. It's what you need to do. You need to let it out.

"But it's been years . . ."

Do it for me. Do it for yourself.

I blink back the rushing peel of warmth at the back of my throat.

Just tell them. Okay?

I nod.

I've gotta go.

"Where to?"

Home.

"We can go together," I tell him.

A light, dazzling and hard, shines in my eyes . . .

"Take the light away," I scream. "Take it away. I need to see Jem." A siren shrieks. Darkness, soft and warm, enfolds me.

"Jem."

Take care, kiddo.

The roaring in my head fades. It stops banging against my brain. I pull in a long deep breath, push open the window and lean way out. Mom and Dad are talking in hushed voices. Somewhere. They sound close. The softly falling rain smells a bit like the sea after a storm. Clean and salty. I'm walking along the shell path in bare feet after Trace dared me.

My feet bled. My blood left little rusty pinpoints on the white, gleaming path. It had been initiated.

"She moved. I saw her head move."

Of course I can move, Dad.

A pain pulses. Jerks me.

A gasp. A long sucking in of air.

Crying. Someone's crying. It can't be me. I never cry. Besides there's nothing to cry about. Jem's fine. He's just fine.

chapter thirty-three

"Zara, can you hear me?"

Where's the blue door? Where's Hoodman and Dark Eagle?

My eyes fly open.

I stare into a young face with small eyes and smooth blond hair. He is leaning over me.

"Can you hear me?"

I open my mouth but it is too dry to speak.

"It's all right, Zara. You're safe. You've been in a coma."

No, I want to say, I've been off finding Jem.

"There was an accident."

"Get out of the way, kid," Jem had yelled. We swerved, skidded sideways. The singing tires turned into a high-pitched shrieking sound. The tree was there at the front of someone's yard, and the parked car.

I screamed as I flew at the window. And as my face smashed into the glass I felt Jem slip away, disappear from his beloved bike.

I pull off the thing covering my mouth. "Jem?" I whisper.

Mom nods. Clings to my hand.

Dad shakes his head.

"No," I whisper. "He's fine. I just saw him."

The doctor speaks. "It's going to take a while."

"It's all my fault. If I hadn't gone on and on . . ."

"Shush," says Mom. "None of it was your fault . . . none of it . . ."

I lie there staring upward at the ceiling. Try to pull myself into it. Take myself away from what they've just told me, away from the truth, like I did when I was seven.

My eyes fill with moisture. Far off, I hear music. It is gentle and sweet. It swells inside my head. My tears fall without a sound onto the pillow. This time I don't bite my tongue; I don't stop them.

chapter thirty-four

"Hey, girl. You scared us shitless. Lying there day after day like that. You had us all wondering at times."

I grin. Sitting propped up against the pillows. Listening to Trace. Smelling the last of the autumn, feel it drifting in the window.

"Anyway, you've simply gotta hear all about the pop-idol thing that's been happening at school. What you missed." She rolls her eyes.

"I like your face," I tell her before she can launch forth. The Goth has gone. It's been replaced by a shining, clean look.

"What, this old thing?" Trace gives a half-embarrassed smile. "Yeah. Well. It's all Blondie's fault. That's me in the contest. You want a drink?" She holds up the jug.

I shake my head. The pillows rustle.

"Always so damn hot in this place." She fills up the glass with the orange juice left by Mom. Drinks it straight down. "You know that Paul came in heaps to see you?"

"Mom told me."

"So you'd better do something about it when you get out of here."

"Give us time."

Trace grunts.

"Okay. Okay. I will."

"Good. Because if you don't . . ."

"Tell me about you and Blondie," I interrupt, settling deeper into the pillows.

"See, I wasn't ever going to go in for something so stupid as being a pop idol, but then I did. It all started when that dork Rodney put my name down and I didn't see it until it was too late."

I close my eyes, let Trace's words drift around me, while she tells me about the pop idol contest.

"Hey! You listening? Or are you drifting off?"

I flick open my eyes. Turn to face Trace. "Bit hard not to listen."

"Oh, ha-ha. Thanks very much." She bends over and digs around in her black bag. Pulls out her staple food. Rips open the bag of onion chips. "You want one?"

"I'm fine. So when's the big finale?"

"Tonight."

"You shouldn't be here. You should be rehearsing."

"Shit, girl. You come first. You should know that by now."

A quiet feeling swells at the back of my throat. Moisture rims my eyes. I blink hard. I don't want Trace to think I'm going soft.

"What are you singing?"

"'One Way or Another.'"

"Good choice."

Trace shakes her head.

"What?"

"It's not a good choice. It's a freakin' great choice." She laughs. Crinkles up the empty bag and tosses it into the bin.

"Hi there, you two. What are you hatching?" Aunt Chloe comes into the room. Under her arm is a large parcel. She places the package on the bed. "For you, honey."

I push myself up. Ignore the sudden stab of pain in my leg. "What is it?"

"How about opening it to find out?" says Trace.

I ignore her sarcasm, untie the ribbon, and fold

back the silver paper. Inside lies a sketchpad, several pens, and pencils.

"What do you say?" says Aunt Chloe with a smile. "Think you could manage to do some drawings? Even though I know your arm isn't the best. It might keep you from getting into mischief while you're stuck in here."

I know I can, but I'm not sure I want to. It feels as if that part of my life is finished, cut off with the death of Jem. Anything to do with before the accident is somehow blank, gone.

"Thanks. They're great."

"You don't have to use them. Not right away. Just when you feel like it." Aunt Chloe's disappointment hovers.

"I will," I tell her. "Truly."

The lie is there ready to be built upon. A pale gray fib, not yet dark enough to be seen, but waiting for the next one, and the next until I'm ready to be honest with myself and others.

Aunt Chloe nods. "In time you'll want to, I'm sure."

"Okay, girl," says Trace, collecting her bag from beside the chair, "time I shoved off. Need to fix myself up for tonight."

"Don't forget to give it all you've got and then some."

She grins. "No worries about that. Blondie's already pulsating."

"Good luck," says Aunt Chloe.

At the door Trace pauses as if wanting to say something else, then she changes her mind. Waves, and dives off down the corridor.

Yeah, me too, I think, picking up on her thought. Wish I could be there as well.

It's been two days since I came out of the coma. Two days to let myself understand and remember what happened. That split second of awfulness before we crashed and knowing Jem had been killed. That he died on the spot, and that I was flung into a car, into the side window. Down and down through glinting, sharp fragments until there was nothing left. Voices, people shouting, and someone kneeling beside me asking if I could hear them. I tried to tell them I was okay, except for my leg and right arm and the prickling in my head and face. I heard the ambulance's siren screaming, the dazzling light shining in my eyes, then there was nothing except a warm darkness.

I'll be in the hospital for ages yet, but the splinters of glass are all gone from my face. I've stitches everywhere. My arm is battered and bruised, but it will be okay in time and they've told me I'm lucky I didn't lose my right leg. They've told me more than once that I'm lucky to be alive.

chapter thirty-five

It's early evening.

Mom and Dad are here. They both seem awkward. I try to let them know I'm okay. I know it's to do with Jem. I haven't said anything about him. I can't. It feels too raw. Like a knife has slashed him out of my life and the hole is still wide open, gaping, bleeding.

But I will. And when I'm ready I will tell them about that other business when I was taken. I made a promise to Jem and myself, and it's one I'm going to keep.

"Dad's done a wonderful job with the garage," says Mom. "It's almost finished. It was so kind of everyone to help us. Donate the wood and iron and whatever else was needed."

I nod, not saying anything. Mom told me all about it yesterday; she seems to have forgotten.

"After all this time. Funny the things that seem unimportant for a long time suddenly become important. Jimmy Mulholland gave a hand."

"He made great cups of tea." Dad's smile leans in a haunted and tired way across his face.

"Are you selling the house?"

"Whatever gave you that idea?"

I shrug. "The garage has been like it has for years . . ."

"No. No." Mom's voice is almost fierce. "It needed to be done. That's all."

To keep them from thinking about Jem and me. I can't imagine what they've been through, knowing I could die as well.

Mom changes the subject. "Trace came second in the contest, but don't tell her I told you. She's coming in later."

"She'll be totally impossible now."

Mom and Dad laugh.

Then Dad says, leaning forward, "Now, here's something you'll never guess in a million years."

"What?"

"You're going to have a cousin."

It takes a moment for the meaning to sink in. "You don't mean Aunt Chloe . . ."

Dad nods. "Phoned, just as we were leaving. Wanted us to share the news with you."

The three of us grin at each other.

"What happened to the corporate ladder?"

"Seems like she left it for a bit to do something else."

"Bill," says Mom in a mock scolding tone.

I laugh.

And I feel a pinprick of rawness ease.

chapter thirty-six

I pick up the comic—the last one Jem bought—
and flick through the pages. There's Hoodman and
Dark Eagle, and for a moment they seem almost
real. Then I close the pages, add it to the pile on his
bed. They've been sold to a collector. To someone
who's as crazy about Hoodman as much as Jem was.
I know he's the right person. It's what Jem would
have wanted. The money's going to be used to help
me get into Holland Art College. But only if I get
one of their scholarships. But it's not happening
yet. Not until next year. Or who knows. It might
even be the one after that. It really doesn't matter.

I wander through to my bedroom and over to
the window. Snow covers everything. The trees look
dark against the bright glare.

Paul's coming over this afternoon. We're not
exactly going together, but we are, if you get my
meaning. It's not written in ink; the rules can be
changed. That way it keeps us both free. Not that

I'm letting any other girl near him, mind you.

I open my sketchbook and let my pencil skim over the whiteness. There's Jem looking up at me and laughing from the snowy garden. He's pointing to his bike, which is all shiny and bright.

How are you doing, kiddo?

I'm doing okay, I tell him. I've still got some way to go, but I'm coping. And get this . . . I've got a limp. Most impressive. The doctor said I'll probably have it for life. Better than losing an arm or hand, though. A limp I can deal with. My face is healing. It's not ugly or anything, just traces of where I smashed into the glass. Memory scars sewn into my skin. Hopefully in time they'll fade. If not, there's always surgery.

When I glance back down into the yard, Jem's gone.

Soon it'll be spring. That's when Trace and I are taking off. Me to check out the art college in the big bad city and Trace to give her opinion of the malls.

For now, though, I am happy just being right here.

Aunt Chloe was right. I do want to draw. It's all I've ever wanted. It's me.

THE DAILY TIMES

MAN TAKEN IN FOR QUESTIONING

A local businessman is helping the police with their inquiries in regards to an incident in the High Street Park earlier in the month. Police have not yet released the name of the suspect at this stage.

In a statement Chief Constable Stevenson said they were not yet willing to confirm that this particular person had been of interest to them for several years.

The young girl in question was unharmed.

Investigations are ongoing and this time police are confident of a successful outcome.